Bitter

By

Bridgette I'esha

Bridgette I'esha

Acknowledgements

First and foremost, all thanks go to the man above. Without him in my life, none of this would even be possible right now.

My parents: Thank you both for believing in me and encouraging me along the way. Love you both to pieces.

To my publisher Tiece: Thank you for giving me the chance to pursue my dreams. I really do appreciate all the support and help you give. You're always motivating the team to go hard! You the real MVP!

To everyone in Write House and Tiece Presents/ Miss Mickens Presents: Thank you for all the love and support   you   show. This   squad has nothing   but hardworking hustlers with serious pen games!

To my little sisters Ti& Mikayla: Love you both!

To my sons Jerome III (Lil' Rome) &Jahsiem (Siem): Everything I do is for you two! Whenever I feel like giving up, I look at both of you and remember it's not an option. Mommy won't stop grinding until you two have the good life you deserve. You two have made me into the woman I am today. I wouldn't trade you two for anything in this world. I love you to the moon and back!

Bridgette I'esha

To Jerome Jr. (Rome): My husband, best friend, and love of my life! Thank you for supporting me all the way, for understanding my late nights and early mornings, and for motivating me when I tend to slack off in my writing. I love you more than words can describe.

To all my family and friends: (It's too many of y'all to name every one of you individually), I love you all and thanks for all the support!

Lastly to my readers! Thank you, all for the love, and support you show me, I really do appreciate each one of you.

Prologue

Sanai

Once again, it was the first of the month which meant it was time to pay bills all over again. I sat Indian style in the middle of my bedroom floor going over old receipts and shredding them. I had so many shoeboxes piled up to the ceiling it was ridiculous. With all the businesses we had going on it was becoming hard to keep everything organized. I felt like I needed to hire a personal secretary to help me with this mess. Knowledge was gone, and the kids were at school, so this was the only free time I had to get anything done.

My bedroom was so spacious, and I loved it. When Knowledge first had the house built from the ground up, we both decided we needed our own bedrooms and offices built. With all the clothes and shoes, we had, we needed the extra space. The black curtains hanging up to the window blocked out all the sunlight, which made the room more relaxing. Marilyn Monroe was the decor throughout the entire room. She was my inspiration in life.

As I went through a few bills, I noticed a few pictures of Asia tucked away in the shoeboxes. At first, I thought nothing of it until I continued to find more pictures of her. I threw them off to the side with the receipts when something grabbed my attention. On the back of one picture read, 'To my daddy, from your princess Asia'. Now if it had said Uncle Knowledge or God dad Knowledge I wouldn't have been so suspicious, but the shit clearly said daddy, and it was written in Jade's handwriting. I was so furious I began kicking boxes left and right. One of those muthafucka's had some explaining to do. I pulled my weave up into a tight messy bun, greased my face real good with some Vaseline, and put on my butter Timberland boots. The only thing on my mind was whipping somebody's ass. I didn't even bother locking up the house as I rushed to my truck. I sped in and out of traffic going well over the speed limit.

When I pulled up to Jade's house, anger took over my body. In the driveway was Knowledge's black Lexus LS460. He was the only one around town who had that car. The first thing I did was grab the knife I kept hidden underneath my seat. I got out the truck and walked over to Jade's car. I stuck the knife in each tire and watched the tires as they deflated. Once I was sure all the air was out, I did the same thing to Knowledge's shit. I knew I should've been taking the shit out on Knowledge, but Jade was my best friend, and some shit you just didn't do out of respect. I was glad they didn't hear any of the noise I was making. I wanted to see the looks on their faces when I caught them dead in the act. I used the spare key Jade kept hidden under the welcome mat to let myself in. To my surprise, nobody was sitting in the living room, but I could hear a heated conversation coming from the back of the house.

"Knowledge I'm sick and tired of having to keep our daughter a secret."

"Don't start that shit up Jade. You know damn well I can't broadcast to the world I have a child by my girl's best friend. How the fuck will that look Jade? Come on now, use common sense."

"It'll make you look like the cheating ass nigga you are."

"No, it'll make you look like the thirsty ass bitch I always told Sanai you were. Who the fuck rapes niggas? Oh, I forgot, ya thirsty bum ass. You'll never amount to be half the woman Sanai is. I don't give a damn how much you blackmail me, you'll never be a part of my life and there will never be an us."

"You and Sanai both can suck my ass, straight like that. I never liked her ass anyway. Always bragging about what Knowledge does for her. I wonder how she would feel if she knew you loved to give me kisses down below."

"Now you know damn well that's a fucking lie!" Knowledge said, jumping up and into Jade's face.

"I know that, but she doesn't," Jade smiled, folding her arms with a devious grin on her face. I wanted to punch her dead in her face, but I needed to hear more. Jade was digging herself one big ass hole and she didn't even know it. The more she talked, the more her true colors were revealed. This bitch had been jealous of me from the beginning. I stood there and kept listening. She was liable to slip up and say some more shit that wasn't supposed to be known.

"You know something Knowledge? I had a thing for you ever since I first laid eyes on you. I ain't gonna lie, I was mad as hell when you chose Sanai instead of me. I mean, her ass ain't fatter than mine," Jade said, removing the plush pink bathrobe from her body. "And I know her pussy ain't tighter than mine," she added as she stuck two fingers inside of her twat. That was it. I had seen and heard enough.

"You trifling bitch!" I yelled, tackling her like I was a football quarterback. I sent blow after blow to her face. I made sure to put rings on each one of my fingers before I left the house. I was determined to leave my mark somewhere on her body. "How could you do this to me Jade?"

She laughed like what I said was a fucking joke. The blood dripping from her nose was getting all over the white carpet, which I was sure my man's money had paid for. Jade might have made decent money taking off her clothes, but she didn't make enough to afford the finer things. When I spit the razor from out of my mouth, which I kept hidden under my tongue, the smile on her face quickly faded. I spit that bitch out so fast I ended up leaving a nice size gash on the side of her face. She wouldn't be prancing her ass around the club any time soon.

" Sanai, baby chill the fuck out!" Knowledge begged.

"Nigga, you didn't tell ya dick to calm down when you were fucking this nasty bitch did you?" I asked, waiting for him to reply with some stupid remark so I could gut his ass like a fish.

Jade was bleeding out bad, but I didn't give a damn. For all I cared that bitch could've died right there. Knowledge grabbed my hand and that's when I turned around and swung my blade. Instead of slicing his face, I ended up cutting a good chunk of his arm. Jade was my best friend, but since Knowledge was my man he was the one who owed me loyalty.

"I hope you didn't think you were getting off scot-free."

"Sanai, let me explain."

"Knowledge what is there to explain? You have a baby by my best friend. There ain't much you can say about that."

"I'm sorry Nai," he said, calling me by the name he had given me years ago. The funny part about it was he only called me that when he knew he had fucked up. As far as I was concerned, my work here was done. I kicked Jade in the face one more time for good pleasure. She and Knowledge could enjoy being one big happy family.

"Knowledge don't you dare bring ya ass home tonight."

"You not about to keep me from seeing my kids," he replied.

"I never said anything about Justice and Jordan. What I said was don't bring ya black ass to the house."

"Watch me," he said like I was playing some kind of game. I was dead ass serious. There was no telling what I would do, especially since I wasn't in my right state of mind. I guess I would have to make an example out of his ass if he showed up.

"Don't try me Knowledge. I'm not through with your ass yet so don't make this harder than what it's got to be," I said, brushing past him.

I called Paris to inform her of what had gone down, but her phone kept going straight to voicemail. I wanted her to know about the bitch she had been calling her best friend for years. Out of all the bitches in the world, Knowledge got her ass pregnant. His ass was so damn dumb he hadn't even bothered to get a DNA test done. I didn't care how much they said Asia looked like Justice, which she did, everybody knew the longer you fed them the more they looked like you. I wanted to turn around and set that damn house on fire. I wanted both of them to burn! Just when I thought Knowledge was a changed man, I get hit with a ton bricks. I couldn't blame anybody but myself though. I was doing wifey shit for a fuck boy that wasn't ready to commit to nobody but his money.

Since I couldn't get in touch with Paris, I called Kobe. I knew she would love helping me torture Knowledge's ass. She knew him as well as I did. It was crazy how we had developed a relationship despite our circumstances. Knowledge and I had been taking one of our mini-breaks when I found out about Kobe. She made it her personal business to inform me about her and Knowledge's affair. I couldn't even fault her when she told me everything. She had come at me like a woman, and not on that disrespectful shit. From there on out we had formed some sort of friendship.

The phone rang for a little while before she picked up.

"Hello?"

"Kobe, its Sanai."

"Hey what's up?"

"I know you down to help me fuck some of Knowledge's shit up?"

"And you know this boo! Where you need me at?"

"Meet me at the crib. Put on some clothes you don't mind getting dirty. And be sure to bring bats, I know you still keep some in your trunk."

"Do I need to put on my steel toe boots?" Kobe asked. "I like to be prepared at all times."

"Yeah, I already got my shits on laced and tight."

"Damn, what has his ass done now?"

"This nigga done had a baby by Jade's ass," I said, refusing to believe this shit was true.

"Not ya best friend Jade?" Kobe asked.

"Yes, that bitch."

"I wished you would've said that shit from the beginning. Let me throw my hair up in a ponytail and I'm on my way."

"Bet. By the time you get there I should be pulling into the driveway." I hung up the phone and headed to the house. Knowledge and Jade had just awakened a sleeping beast.

Knowledge

I knew Sanai's ass was crazy, but I didn't think she would cut a nigga, and she had cut me good. Luckily, it wasn't bleeding as bad as I thought it was. I ripped off a piece of my shirt and wrapped it tightly around my arm. That would stop the bleeding until I got medical attention. Jade had managed to disappear to somewhere, I didn't know where to. All this bullshit was her fault. I knew I should've just told Sanai from the beginning, but knowing Sanai, it would've been much worse. I didn't know how much of the conversation she had heard, but I hoped it was enough to plead my case. It wasn't like I fucked Jade on purpose. The bitch had been plotting on me from day one. I didn't know why she wanted me so bad. As much as I cheated on Sanai I should've been the last man she was attracted to. She knew firsthand the drama we went through in our relationship, yet she was still pressed about me and her being together. No matter how many times I told her it would never happen, it never seemed to register.

When I got outside, I noticed my car was sitting down extra low. "The fuck!" I yelled out. Sanai had flattened all my tires and Jade's too. I sent a message to all my boys letting them know I needed them. A few minutes had passed and still no one had responded back quick enough for me. I took off walking down the road. I wasn't walking a good ten minutes when an all-black Suburban pulled up in front of me, followed by two silver Hummers. I couldn't see who was inside due to the tint on the windows being so dark. I reached into my pockets only to come up empty handed. The day I didn't have my burner on me I was surrounded by a couple of vehicles. I jumped back a little when the door on the Suburban opened.

"Get in," I heard a voice say. I didn't move as I let the voice register inside my head. When it finally clicked, I was being pulled into the truck.

"Juju?" I asked, trying to make sure my eyes were seeing things correctly.

"Yeah it's me baby. Alive and in the flesh."

Seeing Juju alive had me madder than a muthafucka. How could he be alive all this time and not tell me. Shit I was supposed to have been the one nigga he could trust, and here he was with truckloads of niggas. This shit had my ass feeling some type of way.

"Why you over there looking all tight and shit?" Juju said as he lit a Cuban cigar. He was acting like there was nothing wrong with him just reappearing out of the clear blue.

"Where the fuck you been at all this time? You didn't think about letting ya lil bro know that you were really okay."

Juju took a long pull from the cigar; it was obvious that life was still treating him good. He had on a pair of fresh Prada shoes and the matching shades to go with it.

14

"I've been around watching you. Trying to see if you've been handling the operation like you were supposed to, and I must say that I'm highly impressed. You showed me that everything I taught you wasn't in vain."

"I paid attention to the best," I said boosting his ego a little bit. I decided not to give him a hard time at the moment. I wanted to know what made him come back. "What brings you back around? I mean you have been gone for almost three years."

"I've been watching Trina's snake ass for the last year. The same niggas she been running around with were the ones who robbed me that night."

"What do you plan on doing about that bitch?" I asked disgusted by everything. I was ready to put in some work. That nasty bitch had damn near cost my brother his life. She was still living in his house reaping the benefits that came from being his girl. If it was my call, I would've just put a bullet in her head, but since it was my brother's bitch, I was gonna sit back and let him call the shots. If he was still letting Trina breathe all this time, then he must've had a plan for keeping her alive.

Paris

My phone vibrated on the desk. Whoever was calling would just have to wait. I was in no mood to have a conversation with anybody. I just wanted to get some rest and be left alone. Romeo had left to handle things, so I was alone in the room enjoying some me time. Romeo was truly an angel in disguise; every time I turned around, he was right there coming to my rescue. Legend had truly showed me a side of him that I never knew existed, and I

was scared. All this drama with Legend was taking a toll on my sanity. I prayed every night asking the Lord to show me away from it all. Just the thought of Legend almost raping me brought tears to my eyes. I was more than positive he would stop at nothing to make my life miserable. Not only had he cheated and gotten another bitch pregnant, but he had told me to my face that he fucked my best friend. I couldn't lie, I was hurt. I really expected more from Jade. I had really considered her a friend these years. Even for her that was a low blow. The stomach pains from not eating anything had started to kick in. I pulled out the menu to see what room service had to offer.

"Room service, what can I get for you?"

"Can I get the lobster tail and T-bone steak?"

"How would you like your steak cooked?"

"Well done, with no pink at all."

"And what would you like for your sides?"

"Fresh broccoli and a baked potato."

"Is there anything else I can get for you?" the operator asked.

"Yes, a side of cocktail shrimp and some A1 steak sauce, and please cook my steak with onions."

"No problem ma'am. Your order should be ready in about thirty to forty-five minutes."

"Okay, thank you," I said and hung up the phone. Romeo still had a bottle of 1738 by the bed so there was no need in my ordering any alcohol. I didn't drink brown liquor, but I needed something to take away the pain I was feeling. No matter how I looked at it, I couldn't believe that I had been betrayed by my best friend. I ran some hot water in the heart-shaped Jacuzzi tub. I figured I could soak for a few minutes while I waited for my food to arrive. Fifteen minutes later, I was out of the tub. It had gotten too hot for me to stay in there any longer. After I dried off, I changed into some comfortable clothes, a wife beater and some tights. I tied my hair up and flipped through some channels on the television. Nothing good was on except an old episode of *If Loving You Is Wrong*. I was just getting into the show when there was a knock at the door. *Damn that was quick,* I said to myself. When I opened the door, I was petrified. Legend stood there with one hand behind his back. He bum rushed me inside the room, leaving the door wide open.

"Paris, won't you just make things easy on yaself and come on home. I'm growing tired of playing these fucking games with you," he said as he circled around my body with the gun pointing at my head. I didn't say a word as I laid there. I was truly scared for my life. It was clear that Legend wasn't in his right mind. Something inside of him had snapped. If I said one wrong thing, you would've probably been hearing about me on the six o'clock news. I said a silent prayer hoping that God would at least answer this prayer.

"Now we can do this the easy way or the hard way, it's your choice. Now I want you to get up and follow me out this door. Try anything stupid and I won't hesitate to blow ya fucking head off," Legend said.

I got up from off the floor and did as I was told. We were halfway out the door when Romeo came out of nowhere. He charged at Legend and they both fell to the ground. Romeo struggled to get the gun from out of Legend's hand. In the process, the gun fired off.

Pow! Pow! Pow!

I felt a warm sensation taking over my body as I fell to the ground. I was sure I was paralyzed; I felt no pain and I couldn't move my legs. A pool of blood oozed from the side of my mouth. Was this my punishment for killing a child that I didn't even give a chance at life? Or was it my punishment for being a bitter bitch? I felt like the world was closing in on me as I struggled to take a breath. My eyes closed and before me was my baby girl Sharde standing at that bright light that everyone talked about. Tired of living in the outside world, I reached my hand out to go with her. Finally, my heart and mind would be at peace.

Chapter One

Paris

I woke up surrounded by all my loved ones. I didn't recognize where I was until I heard the beeps coming from the heart monitor. I cried on the inside as I thought about all the events that had transpired in my life in just a matter of months. I couldn't understand why God kept allowing such things to happen to me. But I knew not to question his work. I grunted in pain as I struggled to sit up in the hard hospital bed.

"Be careful baby," I heard my father say as he came running to my side. With the current mess going on between him and my mother, I was surprised to see him here. I snatched my hand back when he tried to touch me. I couldn't stand to be around a man that cheated. My hate for Legend was turning into a hate for all men that did their women wrong. I watched my father turn to my mother, who in return shrugged her shoulders.

"I got it," I said struggling to sit up. The pain grew as I tried to sit up for a long period of time.

"I'm glad you're okay Toddles, I thought we had lost you," he said breaking down in tears. My heart softened up a bit. My father was a man who rarely ever showed any emotion. "I love you Paris and don't for one second think that I don't."

I dropped a few tears of my own. I couldn't remember the last time I'd heard him say those words. My mom was even in the corner crying.

"I love you too dad," I said meaning every word. My father had always been a part of my life, but he was never there for me. I never felt like we shared that father daughter relationship that most girls dreamed of, which was one of the reasons I found myself in Legend's arms. He filled that void that I was missing. He gave me the love that I didn't feel like I received at home. Legend gave me the attention that I wanted from my father. To me, he always focused more on his career than his family. He stayed gone all the time, so it wasn't much of a surprise when my mom mentioned them getting a divorce. He reached over and planted a kiss on my cheek. I sat there and cried like a baby. I was an emotional wreck. I was glad when a knock at the door interrupted our family intervention. My ribs were hurting from all the crying I was doing. The doctor walked in carrying her clipboard. My heart thumped rapidly in my chest. I was uncertain about what news she would give.

"How are you feeling?" the doctor asked. She was a real heavyset woman. If I had to take a guess, I would say she was in her mid-forties, but she looked good for her age.

"Like I can't feel my leg," I replied. I could feel the pain in my back but when it came to my leg, I felt nothing. "That would be from the pain medication that I gave you. Let me know if you're experiencing pain in any other places."

"My back is on fire."

"I'll get you some more pain medication once we go over a few things," she said looking over her clipboard. She was taking a long time to get her words out which had me thinking something was wrong. I took a deep breath as I prepared myself for the worst.

"Well for starters, the gunshot wound in your leg damaged quite a few nerves. So, prepare yourself to feel some type of numbness or burning sensation from time to time," she said. I was relieved to hear that I wasn't paralyzed. I figured I would just take some pain pills and be right on my way.

"Okay, I can live with that."

"Wait, there's more." The doctor took her thick framed glasses from off her face and grabbed my hand. "I'm sorry, but there's no easy way for me to say this." She paused a few seconds before continuing.

"Unfortunately, you may never be able to have children. The gunshot wound you experienced to the abdomen caused serious damage to your reproduction system." Hearing those words triggered something in me, which caused me to snap. I began screaming at the top of my lungs.

"You're a liar," I screamed trying to attack her. I refused to believe what she said was true. My mother tried to console me, but I released my anger out on her.

"Get away from me," I shouted. I knocked over the 'Get well' cards that sat next to the bed. I continued with my rampage until the doctor doped me up with some medicine. None of the faces were familiar to me as I wasn't in my right mind. I could only visualize Legend and Jade. Once I got well those bitches were going to pay. I wanted revenge and it didn't matter which way I got it. I would even take it in blood if it meant that vengeance would be mine. They had destroyed my life and now they were going to reap what they had sowed.

"Good morning," I said trying to grab his attention. He was too busy fooling with his phone to hear me. "I said good morning," this time getting a little loud.

"Oh, my bad ma," he said in his deepest voice. The tone he spoke in was so damn sexy. If I wasn't all fucked up, I would've been all over him.

"Ya mom and pops went out to grab some breakfast. They real cool peeps. Ya pops one of them cool old dudes."

"Oh yeah," I said yawning, I was still tired. With all the medicine they kept pumping in me, my body was drained. How long you been up here?" I asked.

"It's been about two hours. But look here, 5-0 has been in and out of here waiting for you to wake up. More than likely, they want to ask you some questions and shit about what happened. Now you can let them get involved or we can handle it ourselves, it's your choice."

I thought about what Romeo had just said and I had made my mind up to let the police do their job. He had done more than enough for me already and I didn't want him to risk his freedom for me. Besides, I knew nothing about the streets. I mean, I smoked weed, but I wasn't ratchet or anything like that. When it came down to shooting people, busting licks and all that other stuff, I was clueless.

"You've done enough." Two detectives walked into the room interrupting our conversation. They waved their badges letting us know which police department they were from. I was pissed. The bastards didn't even bother to knock.

"I'm Detective Roberts, and this here is my partner Detective Williams. We were hoping you could answer a few questions, that's if you are feeling up to it."

I rolled my eyes at the woman detective. The bitch was too busy eye-fucking Romeo to even be concerned with what her partner was saying.

"Okay then. Do you know who did this to you?" was the first question he asked.

"Yes, my ex-boyfriend Legend Dixon."

"Do you know what his motive would be?"

"He's mad about the fact that I've moved on with my life. He's a bitter bitch who's set on destroying my life."

"Do you know his whereabouts? Or anyone he may be with?"

"No, I don't, and I could care less. Any more questions?" I asked. I was ready for them to get the hell out of my room before I went off again. As soon as they exited the room, I started to check Romeo's ass, but I didn't. I couldn't be mad at him when the detective was the one all in his face. He didn't even acknowledge the bitch while she was in here. He spoke and kept it moving so there was no point in making an argument out of nothing. Romeo's gaze met mine and I was shocked to see his eyes watery. I went to go sit up, but was stopped by the pain in my back.

"I feel like this shit is all my fault. I should've went ahead and deaded the nigga the first time. Ain't no telling how you would be if I hadn't come back to the room when I did." He blinked his tears away. I guess he didn't want to cry in front of me and I understood.

"You can't blame yourself because it's not your fault."

"Yo Paris on some real shit, I really care about you a lot. I would've been all fucked up had that nigga took you away from here."

I listened as he spoke and for some reason I could tell he was being genuine, and nowadays that was hard to find. Romeo had been nothing but kind ever since the day he stopped me from taking my life. Now how ironic was that, I was now sitting in the hospital bed alive instead of dead thanks again to Romeo. I didn't know why God sent this man into my life, but I was grateful for him.

"Oh my God! Oh my God! Are you okay?" Sanai's over dramatic ass came bursting through the doors.

"Better days are to come," I said, trying to find something to be positive about.

"I can't believe that son of a bitch did this to you." Sanai was hype and ready to go to war and that's what I loved about her. She would beat a bitch's ass on sight and worry about the consequences later.

"I know, but what's with the outfit?" I asked changing the subject. I was over talking about Legend. The only thing I wanted to hear about him was that he was either locked away behind bars or six feet under. Sanai took a seat in the chair and I could tell something was bothering her. She was never this quiet.

"Can you believe that Knowledge is the father of Asia?" I had to make sure my ears were hearing right. I

looked at Sanai and she verified what she had just said.

"You heard correct. Knowledge fucked that trifling bitch Jade and got her pregnant. I should've known something was off. She had started acting real shady after she had Asia. She acted like we were in competition all the time." Sanai spoke with more hurt than anger in her voice and I had yet to tell her what Jade had done to me. "If it makes you feel any better she fucked Legend also. He told me the night everything took place."

From the look on her face, I could tell she didn't know if I was for real or playing. Jade was low-down. I had been nothing but a good friend to the bitch and she goes behind my back and fucks my ex-boyfriend. It didn't matter that me and Legend weren't together at the time, as a friend some shit you just don't do. I mean damn, it wasn't like she didn't know I had invested years with his ass. But you know that's just how some bitches get down. I don't know why I expected more when these hoes ain't loyal, and a hoe was exactly what Jade's ass was. But she wasn't just an ordinary hoe; she had used everything I told her about me and Legend's relationship to her advantage. That was my fault though. I had trusted a nigga that I knew wasn't shit and a bitch that was scandalous. You see I could respect an honest hoe, but it was the sneaky ones that got under my skin. Knowing Jade, she probably had been plotting for a minute. That was just how she got down. Ugh, the way I was feeling, I would've dragged that bitch around this hospital and stomped her ass out a few times. She had taken this shit to a whole nother level. I counted to ten to calm myself down. That bitch was now number one on my revenge list. I see why she never wanted to tell me who Asia's father was. She knew I would go back and tell Sanai. Jade was a real crude ball for this shit.

"Why you trying to be funny Paris?" Sanai asked. I was in no joking mood. No female deserved to be cheated on. These niggas had the game all fucked up. Didn't they know what one man wouldn't do the next had no problem doing at all. See the problem with these so-called men today is they think it's okay to disrespect a woman but then get mad when they get a dose of their own medicine.

"Admitting that Legend fucked Jade is the last thing I want to do," I said pointing to the frown on my face. Sanai looked like she wanted to break down. Once again, Knowledge had fed her nothing but lies. I only hoped this time she took it as a lesson learned, or else she would continue to set herself up for failure. Sanai may have had a wild side at times, but she deserved so much more than how she was treated. How she dealt with the multiple side children that Knowledge had was beyond me. She was too good of a woman to deal with the stuff that he put her through.

"She just had it out for the both of us," Sanai said wiping her tears.

"For all we know Asia's might not be his. I mean what did he say about it?"

"Check this out. I overheard them having a conversation and Knowledge pretty much said that Jade raped him."

"What! Is that even possible?" I had heard of men being raped, but I found it hard to believe that Jade was capable of pulling that one off. She wasn't the brightest person in the world.

"Apparently Jade raped him while he was drunk, and she admitted to doing so. Shit like this made me wish I would've left his ass a long time ago." Sanai grabbed her ringing phone from out of her purse. She looked at it and threw it back inside.

"I don't know why he won't stop calling. He made his bed now it's time for him to lay in it."

"What's wrong?" I asked.

"Girl, it's nothing but Knowledge's ass. He's been blowing my phone up, leaving messages saying we need to talk," she sighed. Sanai looked tired and stressed out. I could tell the situation was taking a toll on her. There were bags underneath her eyes. It looked like she hadn't had any sleep in a while. Her skin was usually glowing, but today it was dry and filled with pain.

"Hate to interrupt you two ladies, but I'ma go ahead and leave," Romeo said. I had forgotten about him being in the room with us.

"I apologize for not speaking Romeo, I was so busy ranting I never even acknowledged you. I don't want you to think that I was being smart or anything."

"You good, I understand the both of you have some things that you're dealing with. Paris, you need anything before I go? I'll more than likely be back later."

"As of right now I'm fine. Let's pray that the doctor gives us some good news today. I'm tired of being cooped up in this hospital room. It's making me feel depressed."

"If you would cooperate then the doctors just might consider releasing you soon. That's only if you're healing properly." My mouth was wide opened as I stared at Romeo. To be a thug, at times he talked so proper. "What, why you are looking at me like that?" he asked.

"You don't talk like most niggas who hang in the streets. I mean for you to be a lil thuggish, you speak so proper."

"Let me stop you right there. I'm a hustler not a thug, it's a big difference. Money is my focus. I don't go around being a menace to society. I only make examples out of niggas when they get out of line."

I didn't mean to upset Romeo. My mouth had a way of making words sound harsh, when that wasn't the case. He didn't have a formal way of making money, but it provided him with everything he needed and more. Besides the fact that he sold drugs, I didn't know much about him. We had been friends for a while now and I still didn't know where the man rested his head. He was always so secretive about certain things. I only hoped that there wasn't another woman involved.

"I'm sorry, I didn't mean..."

"Don't worry about it, you straight," Romeo cut me off in the middle of my sentence. He said his goodbyes and walked out the door. I only hoped I didn't mess up the one good thing I had going on in my life.

"What was that all about?" Sanai asked flipping through the channels on the television. One thing about her was she didn't mind asking questions when she wanted to know something.

"You know how my mouth can be sometimes."

"All too well," she said laughing. The nurse rolled her medicine cart into the room. She had a few other nurses with her; I guess it was in case I spazzed out again. It was time for them to shoot me up with some more pain medicine. I was growing tired of having all those drugs in my system.

"That's my cue to leave. You'll be in here looking like a zombie in a minute," Sanai laughed.

"You got my number if you need to reach me," she said as she gave me a hug.

"I love you and take care. You know you're like the sister I never had. I wouldn't know what to do without you," Sanai sniffled. Tears were threatening to escape her eyes and she was fighting hard to hold them back. Her phone started ringing again for what seemed like the hundredth time.

"Let me get out of here before this nigga make me get real ratchet inside of this hospital. I'll check on you later."

"Alright girl," I said right before the nurse jabbed the needle inside my arm. Whatever medicine she gave me sent a warm, burning sensation through my body. It wasn't long before I felt like my body was floating on cloud nine. I struggled to keep my eyes open; I was high as a kite. I adjusted myself on the bed so that I could get comfortable. As soon as I found the right position, I fell into the best sleep I had had in a long time.

Chapter Two

Jade

I was on my way out the emergency room when I saw Sanai come running inside. My blood boiled from looking at her. I had to get twenty stitches in my face and here she was still looking her best. I was glad she now knew about Knowledge and I. Asia would finally have her father around her more often. I was ready for her to get the same treatment he gave the rest of his kids, or I would be making his life a living hell. Shit, who was I

fooling; I planned on doing that anyway.

I placed my oversized Prada glasses on my face, along with my baseball cap. I didn't want to be seen in this condition. Sanai had put a temporary stop to my money until my face healed. There was no way Rico, the club's owner, would let me work the stage looking the way I did. But that was okay, if I had to turn a few tricks in my house while Asia was gone then so be it, one monkey wouldn't stop my show. I kept my distance as I followed her down the hall. I needed to know who she was here to see. I waited until she was completely in the room before peeking inside of the window on the door. A smile crept across my face when I saw Paris all bandaged up on the bed. I didn't know what happened to her, but I was praying that the bitch died. I wanted both her and Sanai to hurt the way I did all those years. They walked around like they had the perfect lives and relationships when they were far from it. I rubbed my stomach hoping I was having Legend's baby, then I would have one up on the both of them. To me, it wasn't about having a relationship with Knowledge or Legend. I just wanted Sanai and Paris to see they were no better than me. I didn't need to see anymore. Whatever happened to Paris I was sure Legend was behind it. Paris wasn't the type to have beef with anyone; she was the type of person that stayed to herself. She just happened to get caught up in my revenge. Being stuck under Sanai's ass all the time was her downfall.

Any normal person would've felt bad for hurting an innocent person, only I wasn't normal. If you weren't on my team, then you were against me and that meant I had to treat you like the enemy. I walked outside and searched the parking lot until I found Sanai's truck. I didn't bother checking the parking lot to see if anyone was watching me. I'm sure the cameras would've caught everything anyway. I slashed every one of her tires, the same way she did mine. She'd be catching a cab home just like me.

♥♥♥♥♥

"Thank you," I said to the cab driver as I exited the cab. I had promised to pay for my fare later that night. He was an older African man who owned a few different companies, and from the looks of things, he was holding plenty of money.

"What time should I come by?" he asked.

"Just call me before you decide to come. More than likely I'll be up, if not I'll hear my phone ring." I gave him my number and said my goodbyes. I planned on draining his bank account later tonight. I unlocked my door to find Legend sitting on my couch drinking a beer.

"What the fuck are you doing here?" I shouted. I didn't know what kind of games he was playing, but I wasn't feeling this shit at all. I didn't even play Knowledge popping up at my house when he felt like it, and he was no different.

"Shut the fuck up and come suck my dick." I

turned around to see if someone else was standing behind me. I knew damn well he wasn't talking to me like that. I don't know why these niggas insisted on taking me for a joke.

"Come again," I said.

"Don't make me have to tell you again." He jumped off the couch and walked towards me. I backed up, trying to ease my way into the kitchen. Legend was drunk, and the smell was making me sick to my stomach.

"Don't act like you ain't use to doing this shit. You stay on ya knees for them fuck niggas, why not do it for your soon to be baby daddy?" I cringed when he said that. With him acting like this, I didn't know if I could deal with him for the next eighteen years, but I was too set on hurting Paris.

"The only way I'm getting on my knees is if you're paying. Ain't nothing around here free. Trust and believe I have no problem picking up the phone and calling the police, I'm sure you had something to do with what happened to Paris."

I placed my hands on my hips and snapped my neck, like most girls did when they weren't playing. If they had a reward out for his arrest, then he could forget it. Money always came first in my eyes. It was funny how things worked out. Legend was just about to pop off out his mouth when his picture appeared across the television screen. If he didn't sober up quick when he saw the shit.

"My bad Jade you know I'm just fucking with you."

"Don't try to switch up now, keep talking that shit you were talking a few minutes ago," I said holding the phone in my hand. One wrong move and I was giving the police his whereabouts.

"I need a place to crash at," he said.

"That may be true, but you won't be crashing here. You not about to fuck up the money I got coming in," I said keeping shit one hundred. There wasn't any shame in anything I did. My bills still had to be paid, and his ass didn't even have a job. There was nothing he could do for me.

"Well you need to go crash at your other baby mama house, what's her name? Chanel, Chante, Chantel, whoever she is."

"Come on Jade, don't do me like that," he said on his knees begging. I couldn't lie; I was quite amused by it all. Earlier when I came in the door he was talking shit and now he was kissing my ass. I didn't care how much he begged, he would not be staying up in here. The last thing I needed was for the police to run up in my house behind him.

"Legend, you need to get ya shit and get the hell out of my house." Just like that, he switched his mood had changed. I was beginning to think he was bipolar.

"Keep playing with me and I'ma do you how I did Paris," he said with a smirk on his face. I wasn't sure what he meant by that. All I knew was that Paris was pretty fucked up inside that hospital.

"What you mean by that?" I asked, trying to see if he would elaborate.

"You heard me. Unless you want a bullet in ya chest then you need to start acting right."

I knew then I had no clue what type of man I was dealing with. If he would do that to the woman he was in a relationship with for years, then there was no telling what he would do to me. Immediately I got on my knees and unbuckled his pants. I gave him some sloppy toppy until my jaws locked up. I sucked his little dick like my life depended on it.

"That's right bitch, suck this dick." I moved my head up and down until I felt a kink in my neck. Legend squeezed the back of my neck like he was trying to drain the life out of me. I took his dick and his balls into my mouth at the same time and he went crazy. I thought he was about to have a seizure the way his body was shaking. I almost gagged when I felt his salty cum slide down my throat. I ran into the bathroom to rinse my mouth out. I wasn't about to be walking around with the taste of dick in my mouth. I walked out of the bathroom hoping Legend had left, but he was still in the same spot.

"Look, you can kick it here until later on, but tonight you're going to have to find somewhere else to sleep at," I said running things down to him. I meant it when I said he wasn't about to mess up my money.

"Where am I supposed to go?"

"Like I stated earlier, go crash at ya baby mama spot. Hell, I don't know, make up some shit about you wanting to spend some time with your son." I was trying to come up with any excuse that would get him out of my house. I had some plotting to do and he would only interrupt my concentration.

"That just might work."

"Yeah, get to calling or whatever you must do." I went into the kitchen to get some cleaning supplies, I had to scrub up the dried-up blood on the floor. That would not be appealing while servicing my clients. I was scrubbing the hell out of my floor when an idea popped up in my head. I knew Sanai valued those kids of hers more than anything in this world. Maybe if I kidnapped one of those bastards then she would get the point that I wasn't playing with her. She was gonna pay for the nasty scar she left on my face. I didn't plan on killing one of them, but if I had to, I would. I would have to plan everything out perfectly for it to work. I already knew the kids school schedule from being around them. It would be no problem trying to lure them away since they already knew who I was. When I was done cleaning up my bedroom, I took a seat in the living room to wait for my floor to dry. I could hear Legend on the phone trying to talk things over with his baby mama. I didn't care what he told her as long as it got him out of my house. Legend walked back in the house wearing this stupid ass grin on his face.

"Well?" I asked.

"Well what?" he responded.

"What did she say?" I was asking him questions like he was my man, but I didn't care. Nobody told him to bring his ass to my house in the first place. I was still trying to figure out how he had gotten in without a key.

"I'll be out of here in a few," he said taking a seat back on the couch.

"And you can't leave now because?"

"Look, I said I'll be gone soon so chill the fuck out with that bullshit."

I had to refrain myself from wilding. I didn't know how Paris had put up with his disrespectful ass. A nigga that had no job or money had no business talking reckless to a female period.

"Yeah, whatever." I went into my room and pulled out a cute little lingerie set for tonight. If the cab driver tipped well, I planned on turning him into one of my regular customers. I don't know why I was worried so much about whether my outfit looked right, when everything was all said and done we would both be in our birthday suits. I guess I just wanted to make a good first impression. I had no problems satisfying a man, I was just after the money. I walked into the bathroom and locked the door. If Legend thought he was getting any pussy from me, he had another thing coming. I wasn't even feeling him at all. If I was in fact pregnant by him, I planned on putting him on child support as soon as the baby was born. He was mistaken if he thought I forgot about how he dogged me out after we fucked in the club. He would also face the consequences for fucking me over. I turned the faucet to the hot side and let the water fill up the tub. After making sure the water was the right temperature, I climbed inside of the tub, ready for the hot water to ease every ache in my body. I hoped Legend was long gone by the time I was finished.

Chapter Three

Romeo

I was riding down the highway listening to Meek Mill's "Lord Knows" track. I couldn't lie, Paris had me feeling some type of way about the whole thug comment that she made. I don't know where people got the assumption from that if you sold dope then you were automatically considered a thug. Shit, I was just a nigga out here trying to make a living to survive. I bobbed my head to the flow of the music; he was speaking some real shit in the song.

All I ever wanted was a new Mercedes

Bending off the corner, whippin out the lot

Women love me, but the niggas hate me

How can I lose when I came from the bottom?

Lord knows, nigga Lord knows, nigga Lord knows, nigga Lord knows, nigga Lord knows.

Lord knows all I wanted to do was live the good life, and I wasn't far from it. People only knew what I told them. I never allowed a person to know my every move, including Paris. Most just figured I was a nigga that sold drugs, and that was fine with me. What they didn't know was that I had invested my money into numerous businesses. I was on my way to meet with Mr. Giovanni, so I could sign one last document; then everything would be official. I would be proud to say that I was the owner of my own car dealership. This had been in the making for the last year and it wasn't an easy process. Emorej's Foreign Whips consisted of cars such as Aston Martin's, Ferrari's, and Maserati's. I only wanted to deal with people who held that type of cash. I didn't want to be bothered with petty hustlers who wanted cars for show, but wouldn't be able to afford the monthly payments. I wasn't being cocky or anything like that; I just wanted to be where the money was. I had planned on offering Paris a job as the accountant once things got going.

As crazy as it might've sounded, she was the only person I trusted to handle my money statements. To be honest, Paris was one of the real reasons why I wanted to hurry up and open the dealership. When we first started kicking it, I saw the distaste she had about me slanging dope. It wasn't much for me to say about it, I just loved the fast money. I couldn't see myself working nobody's nine to five, unless I was my own boss.

I circled around the block a few times, just to scope the area out. I could see Frank Giovanni from a mile away smoking on a cigar. It didn't matter where he went, he always had a bodyguard or two somewhere near the premises. Sure, enough there was a black SUV parked at the liquor store across the street. My phone vibrated in the cup holder. Knowledge was blowing my shit up, but he would have to wait. Right now, the business I was tending to was more important than the drama he had going on. Don't get me wrong, Knowledge was my day one and all, but that nigga always stayed in some shit when it came to women. It was time for him to finally do right by Sanai. She had held him down when everyone turned their backs on him. She had even run the operation during the time he was mourning Juju's death. Knowledge needed to get his shit together and settle down, we weren't little kids anymore. It was time for us to take shit to the next level like the boss niggas we were. I was ready to travel the country and do shit I saw the white folks doing on T.V.

I stepped out my Audi TT Coupe; I had purchased it a few days ago as a gift to myself. I felt like everyone should reward themselves when they accomplished a goal.

"Romeo, my man," Frank said dapping me up. He was wearing a bad ass $50,000 Desmond Merrion suit. I know that shit probably sounded gay as fuck, but it wasn't another way to describe what he had on. It didn't matter what the weather was outside, he was always rocking an expensive suit.

"Frankie," I said, not taking my eyes off the suit that he had on. He was gonna have to put me on to his clothing connect. It was no denying that he stayed fresh at all times.

"Come on inside, I've been waiting for you." I nodded my head a few times as we walked through the building. The decorator had done one hell of a job getting every piece of décor I had asked for. There was nothing but Italian art that hung on the walls. It went well with the marble floors. I was contemplating whether I wanted to place a mini bar inside. I wasn't trying to have a potential customer come back and sue me for getting into an accident all because they chose to get behind the wheel after drinking.

"I take it that you like everything that you see so far," Frank stopped in front of my office. He had the key, so I didn't know why he was waiting on my permission to enter.

"So far everything is exactly how I wanted it to be."

"There's something else I would like to show you before entering this room. If you would follow me this way." We walked to the back of the dealership. Frank pushed the up button on the elevator as we waited for the door to open. There were three different levels to the place. The bottom was used as storage to keep all the vehicles in excellent condition. The second level consisted of the sales floor and a few offices that serviced each customer individually. Finally, we had the third floor. It was something that Frank and his wife Sara had conjured up.

"What you up to Frankie?"

"I got this man, relax ya nerves and prepare your eyes to see something so rare." Frank stayed talking slick. He was one cool ass Italian dude. I had met him a few years back through Knowledge and Juju. From the little that I knew, Frank had ties with the mob. Few people could tell that he was a very dangerous man. If crossed, he would swipe out your entire family. As long as you conducted good business and stayed loyal, he was good to you.

When Frank opened the door, I couldn't move. My feet were stuck in one spot. My personal office was setup like an apartment. It had glass floor length windows, with a view showing the entire parking lot. In one corner of the room, there was a camera system with several small televisions. It showed every area inside of the building. I even had my own personal bathroom with a shower inside. I couldn't front, Frank had outdone himself with this one. I reached into my pocket and pulled out a wad of cash. I handed Frank at least ten c-notes for getting shit done, it wasn't much, I just wanted to show my appreciation. Of course, he turned it down, but I wasn't accepting no for an answer.

"Keep your money; you've graced my pockets more than enough. Besides, judging by the grin on your face, I'm more than positive this won't be the last time we shall be doing business together."

"No doubt," I replied. "I'm guaranteed nothing but the best when I do business with you." I signed my signature on the last of the papers. Everything was now official; Emorej's Foreign Whips was a go. The only thing left to do was prepare for a grand opening, which I planned on having once Paris was well and out of the hospital. Even though she wasn't my girl, I was ready to show her the world. She had been through so much in a short period of time. My heart ached when I saw her laid up in that hospital bed. Legend had messed her up both physically and mentally. I listened to her scream and cry in her sleep, begging him not to kill her. Legend's life had been spared, but he wouldn't be walking this earth for much longer. I had put a price out on his head. I wanted him brought to me. I didn't give a damn what condition he was in, as long as he came my way. He had tortured Paris long enough and now it was time to put an end to it, once and for all.

"Congratulations," Frank said as he smacked me in the middle of my back. Had he been someone else I would've went to work on his ass. He was heavy-handed as hell, but I knew he didn't mean anything by it. "You're ready to make money on a whole nother level. I've already got a few clients lined up for you; all I ask is that you don't make me look bad."

"Ain't no way I'm fucking up this good money, I've worked too hard to get to this point." Once things got situated over this way, I planned on expanding to different parts of the horizons. I planned on having my name known internationally. Shit, I wanted that Arab money; that Prince Al-Waleed Bin Talal al Saud money. My phone started vibrating in my pocket again; Knowledge had labeled the call urgent, so I knew something wasn't right. I wrapped up the rest of the meeting with Frank and went to my car. I called Knowledge back hoping he wasn't on no bullshit.

"Yo," he answered on the first ring.

"What's good?" I asked, the tone of his voice had me all confused. He didn't sound like his normal self.

"I need you to meet me at my crib."

"Man, I'm not trying to be in the middle of ya drama when shawty get there."

"What you saying?" Knowledge asked, I couldn't tell if he was playing dumb or if he really forgotten about the shit that went down between him and his ol' lady.

"Sanai was at the hospital, I heard all about the shit you got going on with Jade. Nigga, you need to slow down. Shawty was hurt for real."

"The hospital? What was she doing there?"

"It's been so much going on I forgot to tell you that Paris is in there."

"Word, what happened to her?"

"That bitch ass nigga she used to deal with shot her."

"Man, get the fuck out of here, that nigga ain't built like that."

"I was there when it happened, you know me and shawty been talking for a minute. But, anyway she was in there giving Paris the rundown on what happened."

"I wasn't even calling about that though. We got some more important shit to deal with. Just get here soon."

"Iight bet. I'm leaving the dealership now I'll be there in about twenty minutes."

"One," Knowledge said disconnecting the call. I hit the play button on the touch screen stereo that was in the dashboard. I cut the volume up and finished playing my song. The bass was rocking so hard I felt the vibration in my seat.

Lord knows I'm filthy rich

All this ice is like fifty bricks

Rap niggas throwing hissy fits

I give my bitch a stack just for a Christmas gift

My bitch so bad she on my Christmas list

Remember I prayed, I really wished for this

*To get the crib with the maid and with the picket
fence*

*I'm with some niggas that remember we took risks
for this*

I'm talking risky business, flick the wrist

Lord knows that I repent for this

I felt like a new man leaving out of something I could call my own. I was the type of nigga that wanted to see my whole team eat. I wanted everybody on the same page. I didn't care about who made the most money when there was plenty of money out here for all of us to eat. I planned on helping everybody turn legit, but only if they wanted to. I knew I would lose some people on the way to the top, and I was cool with that. It was time for them to either jump on the bandwagon or get ran over. After putting the car in cruise control, I headed in the direction of Knowledge's house.

♥♥♥♥♥♥

It took me ten minutes to find a spot to park in on Knowledge's block. Normally I would've parked either in front of the house or in his driveway, but it was packed. I rang the doorbell letting Knowledge know that I was here. When the door opened, I didn't know what to say. In front of me stood Juju, alive and smoking a blunt. I squinted my eyes to make sure I was seeing everything clearly.

"Don't just stand there nigga, come in." I did as I was told, still not believing what my eyes were seeing. Juju was dead, there was no way he was standing in front of me. I didn't know what type of games Knowledge was playing, but the shit wasn't funny. The initial shock on my face when Juju opened the door was priceless. I followed Juju into the dining room. Knowledge sat at the head of the table with a blank stare on his face. I guess he was still facing the fact that Juju was indeed alive. Now my only question was why would he fake his own death? He could've at least let his own brother know he was living. Something told me that this shit was deeper than I could imagine.

"You can close ya mouth, it's me," he said, lighting up a blunt. I was happier than a muthafucka when he passed that shit my way. I needed something to help me get a better understanding of this situation. "I called a meeting here today to discuss the reasons for my absence. I know you may not agree with the way I went about things, but all I ask is that you show some respect while I'm talking." Everyone in attendance nodded their heads in agreement, cause he damn sure owed all of us an explanation. I took another puff of the blunt as I prepared myself to listen. In the end, I had a feeling we were about to go to war with some niggas.

"The night I was 'supposed' to have been killed, I knew some foul shit was up. Just about all of you know about the trifling ass bitch I was dealing with named Trina, if not I'm sure you've seen her around before." Juju stopped talking so that he could roll up another blunt. "But anyway, that bitch set me up. She had a few niggas that she claimed were her cousins meet me down at the club to cop some work and that was my first mistake. I never went anywhere without letting someone know. The niggas robbed me of everything I held, including the chain that Knowledge and I share alike. At the hospital, I was pronounced dead, but they never double checked for a pulse. They sent me to the morgue and had me listed as John Doe. It just so happened that Lauren, this beautiful lady right here, helped nurse me back to life. Somehow, she was able to pull a few strings to find an unidentified body that fit the description of mine. I know you all are wondering why I waited so long to reappear, but I had to scope things out first. I had to let everyone really feel like I was gone. I needed to find out who the niggas were that Trina were dealing with. And most importantly, I had to be sure about the role she played in all of this."

Juju had said more than a mouthful. I always knew his baby mama wasn't shit, but I wasn't expecting her to take shit this far. She walked around playing the victim when the whole time she was guilty as shit.

"So, you know who them niggas are?" I asked.

"I have an idea of who they are. One of the niggas drive the black Escalade that's always parked at Trina's, I think that's the nigga she fuckin. He be walking around wearing my chain like it's nothing. But what I'm trying to figure out is how did the shit get passed y'all?" The room got quiet as nobody said a word.

"Fuck all that," Knowledge shouted. "I want to know why we ain't out there blowing these niggas heads off, including that bitch Trina." Knowledge's face was tight when he looked at Juju. It was obvious they had some personal shit they needed to discuss in private. I took that as my cue to excuse myself from the table. Both of them had tempers, and I wasn't in the mood to be choosing sides.

"I'll get up with y'all later," I said as I stood up. This shit was too much for me to digest at the moment. I would have to go home and really relax my mind after dealing with this. I exchanged numbers with Juju so that he could reach me when he needed to. I didn't bother dapping Knowledge up since his mood was still off. If he was mad at Juju for not making his presence known before hand, then I couldn't blame him. I would've been pissed to. When I went to exit the door, I ran slam into Sanai. I was glad to be getting out of there, I knew some shit was about to pop off.

Chapter Four

Knowledge

I thought I would've been happy to have my brother back, but I was growing angrier by the minute. He could've at least told me something. I had gotten the pictures he left on my car window, but that didn't mean much, anybody could've sent that shit over. What hurt me even more was that Trina's slimy ass had something to do with his 'fake death' when I had told him several times that she wasn't shit.

"Lil' bro is there something you want to get off ya chest, we both grown," Juju said as he stared me in my eyes. I wanted to square up and go toe to toe with that nigga, but the way he was all cut up, I didn't stand a chance.

"No disrespect to anyone with what I'm about to say. Fuck all these other niggas in the room, I'm your fucking brother and you didn't feel the need to inform me about you being alive, but here you are giving orders like you running shit. You weren't thinking about nobody but yaself with that bullshit. Momma still mourning ya death and you around the world making moves and shit." I got up from the table and paced the floor. I took my anger out on the wall and punched a hole in it. I kept punching until I felt the skin peel on my knuckles. The blood dripped on the white carpet, but I didn't give a damn. I looked at Juju with fire in my eyes. This nigga really didn't see shit wrong with how he went about the situation.

"Three fucking years have passed, and you pop up expecting shit to be all good. Did you really think that things were going to go back to the way they were? The pain you caused the people you love is unforgiveable. Because of you being gone, momma stresses herself out worrying about me every day." My anger had gotten the best of me. For years, I wondered if things would've been different for me had he still been around. I threw the bottle of D'usee up against the wall to stop myself from knocking Juju's dick loose. I was more pissed that I had warned him about Trina, yet he chose not to listen.

"What did you ever see in that bitch for you to become so blind? You were so sprung she made you lose focus."

"Love will make even the strongest nigga fold. When you truly love someone you'll overlook everything, even if the truth is sitting right there in front of ya face."

I wasn't trying to hear none of that love shit Juju was spitting. Plain and simple, Trina had played his ass for a fool. She had the nigga laying up in the house that she and Juju once shared together. Bitches like her were the reason I felt like I could never commit, you couldn't trust these hoes if ya life depended on it. They would set you up and then spend all the money you had in the stash on the next nigga, and that's exactly what Trina had been doing for the last three years. She was lucky her ass was still breathing.

"What happened to money comes first then these bitches?" I asked right before Sanai walked into the dining room.

"Love? My nigga you can't be fucking serious right now. You were in love with a bitch that had been plotting on you the entire time. I bet the bitch cleared out ya entire bank account." When Juju didn't reply, I knew the answer. I shook my head. He was one of the smartest niggas in the world, yet he had been played by a dumb bitch. As far as I was concerned, it really wasn't much for us to discuss at the moment. For the first time in life, Juju had let me down.

"I wasn't playing when I told you not to bring ya ass home." Sanai grabbed the vase from off the table and threw it my way. I didn't move fast enough, and the shit landed upside my head. From there it was no saving the bitch, all the love I had for her went out the window. When she came charging towards me I gripped her neck real tight. At the time, I didn't give a damn about her not being able to breathe. That was gonna be her last time doing physical harm to my body.

"I hate you!" Sanai screamed through the tears that were pouring down her face. She clawed at my face until I had no choice but to let go. She gasped for air as she fell on the floor. I hated the way things were going between us, and I blamed Jade. If the dumb bitch had never raped me I wouldn't even be in this predicament.

"Get it together Sanai," I said trying to console her. She slapped my arms away and I couldn't blame her. I was the reason for her acting the way she was. She fought until she no longer had any strength. When she collapsed into my arms, I embraced her while she cried her heart out. I ain't even gonna front, I shed a few tears myself. I didn't even have a reasonable explanation for why I cheated on her with the bitches I did. A lot of them just threw the pussy at me so I took it. If Sanai took a nigga back I planned on making shit right once and for all.

"Let me help you out bro," Juju said as he bent down towards Sanai.

"I don't need your fucking help, I got this," I gritted. It would take some time for me to get over the way I was feeling. I wasn't surprised when Juju tried to calm the situation between us. Him and Sanai always had a tight relationship, they took their brother and sister title serious. There were plenty of times when I had to ask myself if Sanai was his blood or me. He stayed down my throat about treating her right. Whenever I would dip off with my other baby mama's, Juju made it his business to go back and tell Sanai. At times he was more loyal to her than he was to me.

"I don't know what's going on with you lil sis, but this ain't no good look. The Sanai I know always carried herself like a boss. This crying and shit over a nigga is for them bum bitches, get yourself together ma." Sanai looked up and stared at the strange man in her face. His voice was familiar, but nothing else was. When she noticed she was in my arms she hauled off and slapped the shit out of me. I could taste the salty blood leaking from my lip. She gave me a nasty glare as she got up off the floor.

"Listen up everybody, Knowledge fucked a bitch I once considered by best friend and had a baby with her." I shook my head as Sanai made our business into a public announcement. "That's right the nasty stripper bitch Jade is the newest baby mama." Her chest heaved in and out. I jumped up, thinking she was ready to attack me.

"Damn bro, you just don't quit do you?" Juju said being sarcastic. I knew I had a long track record of having kids outside of our relationship, but that didn't give either one of them the right to put my business on blast in front of everybody. Juju had a few niggas with him that I didn't know, and I knew nothing about the bitch he had with me.

"Excuse me, but who are you?" Sanai asked with her eyebrows raised. For the first time since being in the house, she noticed we had company. "Better yet, who are these people in my house?" Sanai was in straight bitch-mode and she was not to be played with.

"Sanai, you don't recognize ya own brother? It's me, Juju."

"I don't know who you think you're playing with, but you need to leave my house, and this will be your final warning."

"Knowledge, you not gonna help me out with this one?" I turned my head the other way. I wasn't helping his ass with shit until we sat down and had a one on one conversation. I had a feeling it was much more to the story than he was telling.

"Let me throw a little trivia your way that only Juju would know. For Christmas one year I gave you a watch, what did the engraving say inside?" Juju smiled when she asked the question.

"To the world's best brother, blood couldn't make us any closer." When he said that, Sanai stood there in shock.

"It can't be you, you're supposed to be dead."

"So, we all thought," I said.

"This shit is too much for me," Sanai said as she took a seat at the table.

"I'm Lauren," Juju's lady friend said as she extended her hand out to Sanai. Reluctantly, Sanai shook it.

"Sanai, where do you fit in this picture?" Sanai asked sizing her up a bit.

"I was the nurse who took care of him."

"Hmm, I see. I got to pick my kids up from school, I know I just met you, but you're more than welcome to ride if you want. Maybe then you can help me get a better understanding of this situation."

"Alright, let me grab my purse."

I was confused as hell when I watched Sanai and Juju's sidepiece leave together. Sanai was never this friendly to females, especially not ones she'd just met.

"Welcome home," Sanai said as she hugged Juju on her way out.

"I'm glad to be home sis," he replied.

I waited until I heard the front door shut to start in on Juju. For the moment, I would put my feelings to the side. I was ready to find out what he planned on doing to Trina's ass. I poured a glass of Cognac to loosen up a bit.

"You got a plan or nah?" I asked. I never liked Trina from the jump, just thinking about doing harm to her made my dick hard. That bitch deserved everything that was about to come her way, and I wanted first dibs.

"I plan on doing a popup visit one day while the kids are in school, just to fuck with her head a little bit. Then again, you never know how shit may play out." Juju raised his shirt showing the prettiest chrome .45 I'd ever seen; it had the sickest pearl grip. It had me wanting to go out back and bust a few shots off. I had a fascination with guns, along with a mean collection and aim to match.

"How bout you let me take that up off ya hands," I said, with my eyes still on his waistline.

"Nah lil bro, she ain't for sale, but I will turn you on to my gun connect where you can cop ya own."

'That'll work too," I said.

"Tell me that shit Sanai was talking not true." Juju wanted to know a whole lot for somebody that was saying so little.

"I fucked around and was drunk one night and her best friend ended up pregnant." I swear I was growing tired of everybody bringing up Jade's name. She was a mistake I wish I could take back. You would've thought I wanted to be with the bitch the way everybody was acting.

"You fucked up with that one."

"Like I don't know that. Let's ride through and see what Trina's scandalous ass is up to," I said, using that as an excuse to get out of the house. Juju had me missing out on money.

"Knowledge, I know you better than you know yourself. If you got licks to bust that's all you got to say."

"I don't really do too much of that unless shit get hectic during the first of the month. But with Romeo going legit I'ma have to find somebody to take his spot."

"It's time for you to step ya game up. Selling drugs is for them low-level niggas. If you ready to leave them streets alone, I can show you where the real money is at."

"What you talking?"

"The diamonds are where the real money is, I'm talking so much money the only thing you'll be stressing about is where you're going to hide it all." I knew what Juju was saying had to be true, he was a real nigga. He spoke nothing but the truth.

"Selling dope is all I know, so if you willing to teach me that trade then I'm all for it."

"As long as you're willing to take orders, then I have no problem doing so, but I need you focused. I can't have you distracted all because you want to chase pussy. Whatever problems you are having, you need to go ahead and fix."

"I don't chase pussy," I said, clearing that shit up. I had no problem being faithful I just wasn't trying to be.

"Well it must be chasing you then."

"It's my swag, I'm telling you bro, it be driving these bitches around here crazy." I hit the Dougie on him one time to emphasize what I was saying. We both broke out in laughter. "Do we keep you being alive a secret from mama?" I asked.

"For the time being we should. You know how mama is, she'll be on the phone telling the entire town. I plan on laying low until I handle this Trina situation."

"Iight." He gathered up his crew so that we could roll out. Having Juju back around was gonna take some getting used to.

Chapter Five

Legend

Paris reminded me of a black Sleeping Beauty as she slept peacefully in the hospital bed. I stood over her, unsure of my next move. She would have no peace in her life as long as she wasn't with me. I didn't mean for her to get caught in the crossfire, but maybe she'll come back to her senses and realize I was not playing with her. I meant what I said when I told her 'if I couldn't have her, then nobody will'. I would kill her first before I let another man enjoy what belonged to me. Just the thought of another man touching her made my body cringe. I ran my hand down the side of her face. She stirred a little, but she continued to sleep. I wasn't in love with her, I just didn't want her with nobody else. Thoughts of killing her right now ran through my mind, but it would've been too easy. I wanted to drive her crazy, mentally.

"I have no problem killing you," I whispered into her ear. Her eyes fluttered when she heard my voice. "You're not dreaming, it's me." This time she opened her eyes completely. Her body stiffened up when she saw how close I was to her. "Scream and you'll die." I ran my fingers up and down her body.

"Get away from me," she said, finally growing the

balls to say something.

"Or what?" I shouted. "There isn't much you can do in your condition," I said admiring my work. I snatched the blanket back to get a good look at her body, and when I did I snapped. I started punching her in the face repeatedly. "Bitch, you been giving my pussy away?" I screamed, still throwing punch after punch. The only time she shaved her pussy was when she had either had sex or planned on having sex. Somehow, she had managed to pull the call button. The nurse walked in catching me dead in the act. She tried to pull me away from Paris, which only added to my rage. I took the rest of my anger out on her, giving her the same treatment I had just given Paris. I could hear somebody yelling for security. I walked past the people gathered in the hall, daring one of them to say a word. I made it to my car just as the police were pulling into the hospital. I waited until they were inside before flying out of the parking lot. If they wanted me, they would have to come get me. I drove until I ended up at my baby mama's house. When I pulled up, Chante and my son were outside playing in the backyard. I cut the car off and joined them.

"How is daddy's favorite man?" I said as I threw my son up in the air. It had been awhile since I'd spent some time with him, and I felt guilty. My father had practically raised me so there wasn't any excuse for why I couldn't do the same.

"We need to talk." Chante had her arms folded with a nasty look on her face. I wasn't sure what her problem was. I ignored her ass and continued to play with our son. I would deal with her when I got good and ready. "So, you don't hear me talking to you?"

"Yo, I don't know what the fuck ya problem is, but you can dead that smart ass mouth of yours." I didn't know who she thought she was talking to. She had me fucked up if she thought I wouldn't slap the taste out of her mouth for popping fly.

"Last time I checked this was my house and if I say we need to talk then that's what it is. If you don't like what I'm saying, then you can gladly leave. I didn't tell you to come over here." She grabbed our son and went inside the house. I marched in right behind her, trying to figure out what had her all bent out of shape. I picked my son up from off the floor and placed him inside his playpen in his bedroom. I turned on cartoons to keep him occupied while I dealt with Chante's attitude.

"Chante, I don't know what it is you got going on, but you need to get that shit in order." Even when Chante had an attitude, she was so damn sexy. I walked over to her and pinned her up against the kitchen counter. I damn near fell to the floor when she pushed me away.

"The fuck Chante," I yelled, trying not to put my hands on her. I really fucked with her and wasn't trying to go down that route, but she would learn that I wasn't one to be played with.

"What is going on Legend? I done seen ya picture plastered all over the news. If what they said you did was true, then you got to go." I jumped when Chante grabbed the butcher knife from out of the holder. I had forgotten all about me being on the news.

"What you wanna know?" I asked, looking through her refrigerator for something to eat. She ain't have shit in there but some milk and eggs. I closed the door and waited for her to continue bitchin'. I swear I was getting sick of these bitches by the day. Chante wasn't my girl, so technically I owed her no explanation. What I did was my business.

"What did you do to Paris?" she asked. The way she was acting you would've thought she and Paris were the best of friends.

"I did exactly what the news said, I shot the bitch. Now do you have any more questions?" She wanted to know what happened and I told her. It wasn't no need for her sitting on the counter with tears in her eyes. If she wanted to have sympathy for the bitch, then that was on her.

"I have no idea who you are," she said staring at me. She had no idea that I suffered from bipolar disorder. I had the shit under control until I stopped taking my medicine. I had even managed to keep the shit hidden from Paris. I guess you could say I was a pro at hiding things. When my mother ran off when I was younger, something went off inside of me. I felt unworthy of love from women, all because my mother wasn't there to give me the love that I needed. Paris was the first female I had ever loved in my life. Paris was the one woman who taught me what love was. But when our daughter died she began to remind me of my mother. I felt like she was the reason we didn't have a child. I blamed her parenting skills for her death. I compared her negligence to how my mother wasn't there for me. I knew I was wrong, but that was how I felt at the moment.

"You're right, you don't know me. We just have a son together." I loved the fact that I was getting under her skin. Her face was turning red and her hands were shaking. She needed to be reminded that she didn't run a thing when it came to me.

"She didn't deserve that, and you know she didn't."

"You didn't say she didn't deserve to be cheated on when we were fucking, now did you? I don't recall you telling me to go home when I was over her spending the night." Chante was real funny. Now she had a heart after she had told Paris about our hidden affair. I couldn't do anything but laugh. These bitches were all one in the same. I left Chante in the kitchen while I went into the bathroom to tend to my hygiene. I hadn't been to the crib in a few days and I didn't feel clean at all. When I came out, the smell of fried chicken was lingering in the house. Chante must was ready to forgive a nigga. I went into her closet and pulled out the bag I kept with my spare clothes. I dried off and put on a wife beater and a pair of balling shorts. I flipped through the channels in hopes of finding a good movie to watch. Chante walked in carrying a plate of food fit for a king. She made sure it was piled to the top. I thanked her for the meal she had prepared and sent her on her way. It didn't take long for me to feel tight and full. Before I knew it, I had passed out across the king-sized bed.

♥♥♥♥♥♥

When I woke up, I was surrounded by the damn police. It was at least ten of them muthafucka's in the room with me. "Fuck!" I cursed out loud when I realized that Chanted had set me up. She had fed me real good knowing it would be the last meal I ate for a while. The officers read me my rights as they escorted me into the living room. Chante was in there smiling her ass off.

"Yeah, I was the one who turned you in," she stated. "And I filed for a restraining order against ya ass. Legend, you're not mentally stable and I don't want you around us until you get some help." I was mad as hell listening to the bullshit she was saying. I tried to get at her, but was thrown down to the floor.

"If I wasn't in these handcuffs I swear I would be over there fucking you up," I gritted, she was acting real tough with the police by her side.

"Sir is that a threat you're making?" the officer asked, roughing me up a little bit. He was one of those black cops that loved showing his ass in front of the hunkies. Just to show him I wasn't playing, I hawked up some spit and spat in his face.

"I don't make fucking threats." The cop pulled out his stun gun and tased me a couple of times. The first few shocks had very little effect on my body. When the other cops caught drift of what was going on, they began beating me with their batons. Chante was in the background cheering them on. She was loving every moment of it. I was thrown in the police car and taken down to the county jail.

I was informed of my list of charges and was placed on no bail. I wasn't sweating the charges they were trying to throw my way, I planned on pleading insanity. Once they looked at my health history, I was more than certain I would just do some time in a mental hospital. I used my first phone call to hit Jade's ass up. I wasn't surprised when she didn't answer. She was probably out fucking around. At first, I wasn't going to call my dad. I wasn't in the mood to hear him lecture me about what I had done wrong, but I picked up the phone and called anyway. Just like everybody else, he had seen me on the news. I could hear the hurt and disappointment in his voice. He loved Paris like she was his own daughter. He told me he would be here in the morning to see me, which I knew was nothing but a lie. He had expressed several times before that if I ever got locked up, he would make me sit. I slammed the phone against the wall. I was ready to go to my cell and get accustomed to my new living conditions.

Chapter Six

Paris

When I was informed by the detectives that Legend was behind bars, I breathed a sense of relief. For the moment, I felt like I could finally go on with my life. But even with Legend being locked away, I was still paranoid. I was constantly looking over my shoulder to see if he was ready to pop up from out of the closets or from underneath the bed.

I had two more days left in this hospital and then I would be released. I had no clue as to where I was gonna go. Before all of this had taken place, I had given my landlord the key to my apartment and told her I was gone. She told me I wouldn't get the security deposit back since I didn't give her a full thirty-day notice. At the time, I didn't care I just wanted to rid myself of anything that reminded me of Legend. I knew I could've just gone back to my mother's since she had all the extra space. It wasn't like I didn't already have my own room there. But I knew once I got out she was going to smother me nonstop. I loved my mother dearly, but right now I didn't need all of that as I tried to get myself together. It was gonna take a lot of time for me to get back to my normal self again, but I was determined. I was ready to focus on loving me and enjoying my life. My happiness had been stolen from me, and I was ready to take it back.

Romeo walked in the room looking good as usual. He rocked a black polo, and some Jordan Space Jams, was a tad bit jealous. I couldn't wait to get out of this hospital gown and into some real clothes. "What the hell happened to your face?" he said once he was close on me. I looked away as I relived what Legend had done to me. It was crazy how you could love someone and be with them for years and still not know them. I would've never imagined that Legend would bring so much hurt and pain into my life. I wondered what happened to the sweet man that I once knew.

"Legend came back to finish what he started," I said, still looking away from him. I was too ashamed to look him in his face. I had seen the damage he'd done to my body, and it was far from pretty. Black spots covered my brown skin. The wounds from the gunshot would forever remind me of a man I once loved.

"Say what!" Romeo yelled. "He brought his ass here? I swear that nigga is dead once I get a hold of him." Romeo was pacing the floor, yelling out all kinds of obscenities. I knew he would be pissed when I told him Legend was behind my bruises.

"Calm down, the police arrested him not too long ago," I said to diffuse the situation. I didn't want security to come in and make him leave.

"Calm down? This nigga is really trying to kill you and you're telling me to calm down. Ma, you trippin."

"I didn't mean it like that. I'm trying to save you from getting put out," I said right before the officer on guard came in.

"Is everything alright ma'am?" he asked, while staring Romeo down.

"Yes officer, everything is fine. He was just upset that one of his teams lost." I was glad football was on the television or else I would've looked like a liar.

"Okay then, just keep it down in here." The officer left out of the room and went back to his post.

"Paris, I'll do anything to protect you. Even if that means getting rid of him for good. It's something about you that got a nigga catching feelings and shit. Normally I don't even consider taking bitches serious, and no I'm not calling you a bitch, it's just my way of speaking." I didn't know what to say when Romeo expressed his feelings. A part of me was feeling him too, but I didn't know if I was ready to commit again just yet.

"Don't take what I'm about to say the wrong way. The feelings I have for you are strong, but with everything I've been through, I don't think I'm ready for a relationship this soon. If it's okay with you, I figured we'd just be friends for now and then see where things go from there." I wasn't sure how Romeo was going to take my response. If he decided to go on with his life, then that was cool. I wouldn't expect him to wait around until I decided on what I wanted to do.

"I can respect that," he said as he rubbed on my thigh. The touch from his hands sent chills up my spine. "I'm not the type of nigga that's gonna run to another bitch just because I didn't get the answer I wanted. Anything worth having is worth waiting for. I'm not gonna lie though, if you would've jumped up and said yes, I would've had some crazy thoughts running through my head."

"Like what?" I said giving him the side-eye.

"Like how many other niggas you done said yes to that quick." Romeo always said what was on his mind and I loved that about him. I needed someone who would give it to me straight, whether I got offended or not.

"Whether you believe it or not, besides Legend, you're the only other person I've been with. Before you came along Legend was all I knew. Up until now, I've shot down every man who's ever tried to get with me, so consider yourself lucky." I wasn't sure if he believed me or not and it really didn't matter. My word was bond. Whenever I told someone something it was one hundred percent the truth. I didn't like to be lied to, so I wasn't about to feed anyone else lies. I would tell you the truth even if it hurt you to ya soul. That's just the type of person I was.

"We'll see where this friendship takes us," Romeo smirked. We sat and talked until the nurse came in to give me my medicine. I didn't feel the need to take any more pain pills, but both the nurse and Romeo insisted. They didn't want to see me readmitted into the hospital due to being in pain or moving before I was healed properly. After I was done taking my medicine, I went ahead and explained to Romeo that I had to find a place to stay. He assured me everything would be taken care of by the time I got out. He then told me that he had a surprise waiting on me once I was released. I smiled at the man in front of me. Here we were not even together, and he was always thinking about my well-being first.

"How soon do you plan on going back to work?" Romeo asked.

"It depends on how I feel once I'm out of here." Returning to work this soon was the last thing on my mind, but knowing how easily I got bored it wouldn't be long before I would be calling Destiny and asking when I could start. Being broke was not an option for me. I was feeling Romeo and all, but I was not about to put myself in the situation to have to depend on a nigga. Being with Legend taught me that nothing lasted forever. I loved the fact that I could take care of myself, and I wanted to keep it that way.

"I got a business proposition when you get well, but we not gonna get into all that right now."

"Um okay," I responded.

"Have you spoken with ya home girl?"

"I suppose that you're talking about Sanai, right?"

"Nah, Jade," he said being a smart ass. "Yeah I'm talking about Sanai."

"I haven't talked to her since yesterday. I'm sure she'll either call or come through before today's over with. Why you are asking about her?"

"Nothing," he replied lying.

"Romeo there's nothing more that I hate than a liar. I've been nothing but upfront with you since we became acquainted with one another, so please don't lie to me, that's the quickest way to get you cut off permanently." I was dead serious when I said that shit. If he wanted to know for a reason then that's all he had to say, but that lying shit was dead. He ran his hands across his face and I could tell that something was bothering him. He pulled on his chin hair and let a huge breath.

"Between me and you, Knowledge's brother Juju isn't dead," he blurted out.

"You sure the nurse didn't give you any of my pills. Juju is dead. I went to the funeral myself," I said remembering how close Juju and Sanai had been. She had taken his death hard.

"I'm dead ass. I saw him myself yesterday as I sat in their dining room. I'm not sure what the hell is going on around here."

"Whatever it is, you just be careful. If Juju faked his own death and is back, some serious shit is about to go down."

"Tell me something I don't know already. Just don't mention it until Sanai says something to you about it."

"No problem." Juju being alive didn't have a thing to do with me. Whatever they had going on was their business, and I wanted no parts. I just hoped that Romeo didn't get caught in the middle of it. I knew he and Knowledge were best friends and if anything were to pop off, Romeo would've been right there with him.

Chapter Seven

Jade

"Here you go," the receptionist said as she handed me a card with my appointment reminder on there. "Your surgery will take place exactly four weeks from today. Please be sure to follow any instructions that the doctor may have given you."

"I will, thank you," I said as I walked out of the doctor's office. I had just finished my meeting with the cosmetic surgeon. The scar on my face didn't heal quite how I had expected. I had shown the doctor a picture of Sanai. I told him that's what I wanted to look like when I was done. I wanted to look so much like her that she would fear herself. I wanted everyone to think that I had fallen off the face of the earth while I was putting my plan in motion. I had already put a hefty deposit down to secure my spot. I was getting my entire body made over. Once the surgery was completed, everyone would be like 'Jade who'?

I pressed ignore on my phone as it buzzed. Legend had been calling me every hour since he'd been in jail. It wasn't a damn thing I could do for him. I didn't do jail visits and I damn sure wasn't putting no money on his books. Taking care of grown men was not something that I did. He'd better find one of those female correctional officers to shack up with while he was in there. Legend had become more than I had bargain for. He was used to dealing with those weak women that let him walk over top of them, and that wasn't me. I might've bitched up when he said he would do me the same way he did Paris, but that was only because I valued my life, and he was drunk at the time. Now had he been in his right mind we would've went at it in that house.

On my way home I rode pass the elementary school where the twins went to school. I had been studying their schedule for the past few days. Sanai should've been pulling up any time now to pick up the kids. I threw on my shades and parked a few cars back so that I wouldn't be noticed. It wasn't even five minutes before Sanai was walking up the sidewalk. I could see a female sitting in the passenger seat of the truck. I knew it couldn't have been Paris since she was still in the hospital. I had been keeping an eye on her too.

I recorded the date and time inside the notes app on my iPhone. By time I was through, Sanai was going to feel my wrath. I watched Sanai's daughter Justice come prancing out of the door and it angered me how much my daughter resembled her. My daughter looks like she belonged to Sanai and Knowledge, more than she did me. I couldn't take anymore. I hopped out my car and approached Sanai. I knew it was a dumb move, but I felt the need to taunt Sanai a little bit.

"Oh my, you've gotten so big since the last time I saw you," I said to the little girl.

"Hey Aunt Jade," she responded back. I laughed when Sanai's body cringed at the mention of my name.

"Sanai, when are the kids going to see their sister?" I said throwing it out there. "It's been a minute since they all had a playdate."

"Kids go get in the car," Sanai said as she moved in closer like she was ready to fight. She was falling right into my trap and I was loving it.

"But mommy I want to know what Aunt Jade is talking about," Justice whined, refusing to move her feet.

"Justice, you better get your ass in that car now! And take your brother with you," Sanai shouted. It was now just me and her as we stood face to face, still on the school grounds.

"You better be glad my kids are with me or else I would whip ya ass again and take whatever charges I may get." Sanai had her fist balled up as she stood in my face. I walked closer to her, making it known that I wasn't afraid of her. She might've cut me good last time, but I wasn't' about to back down either.

"So, what you trying to do? I mean we can get it popping right here. It doesn't make me no difference," I said calling her bluff.

"You just better keep your ass away from my kids. When you bring them into the equation, you start playing with ya life. I will kill you over mine and that's not a

threat." Sanai walked off towards her car, but I wasn't finished just yet.

I loved riding the hell out of Legend's dick. I see why you always acted a fool over him with every bitch that he cheated with. It's pretty good. And not to mention the fact that he can suck the hell out of some pussy. I must have struck a nerve with that comment. She had turned around and was charging towards me, only she never got a chance to get any hits in. Whoever the female was that was in her truck came running to her rescue.

"Think about those kids of yours," she said to Sanai. "Now is not the place to do this." She wrapped her arms around Sanai's shoulder and guided her to her truck. Sanai never removed her eyes off me.

"This ain't over! Bitch, I will see you," Sanai shouted.

"And I'll be waiting on you whore," I smiled. My work with Sanai had been completed for the day. She had given me the motivation I need to carry on with my plan.

♥♥♥♥♥♥

I was on my laptop going through my emails. I had setup an account on Craigslist, hoping to bring in some clientele. My pockets weren't feeling as heavy as I wanted them to. I deleted a few messages; some of the emails I had been getting were from old men with sick fantasies. I didn't mind performing the act; my problem was they weren't trying to pay much. My services started at a hundred dollars per hour, and everything about me was satisfaction guaranteed. The only thing about it was they

couldn't come to my house. I made sure to include that they would have to provide a hotel room. I didn't need any of those crazy muthafucka's knowing where I rested my head. I was already taking a risk by meeting up with random men.

One email caught my attention, and from his profile, he lived in the same town as I did. He wanted to meet up tonight, which was fine with me. I replied with my phone number telling him to hit me up with the details of the room. If everything went accordingly, I would be walking out of that hotel room with a big smile on my face. It didn't take long for him to text me with the directions to the hotel. I had at least five hours to get some rest until it was time for me to put in some work.

I then sent my mother a message and told her I would need her to keep Asia for me tonight. Of course, she bitched a fit and told me I needed to sign over my rights since I was failing my daughter as a mother. I couldn't lie, I had been putting so much into getting revenge on Sanai and Paris, I rarely even saw my daughter. It was probably in my best interest to give Asia to my mother. At least I knew she would be in good hands and that she would get the love and attention she needed.

Chapter Eight

Sanai

Today just wasn't my day. Already it had been filled with drama. After leaving from seeing Paris, I get to the parking lot to discover that my tires on my truck had been slashed. So, there I was in the middle of the parking lot trying to figure out how the hell I would get home. Thankfully roadside assistance was included in my car insurance or else I would've been stranded, trying to find a way home. That was first thing this morning and here it was still early in the afternoon and I was dealing with Jade's bullshit. I was growing tired of this girl testing me. She had already fucked my man, what more did she want from me?

If Lauren hadn't been there to stop me from beating Jade's ass, I would've been sitting in somebody's jail cell right now. She just didn't know how close to death she was with that stunt she pulled. It was one thing to play games with me, but when you involved my kids, somebody was bound to get hurt. What grown woman involves children in their pettiness? Knowledge having a child by her was on them. It wasn't like I had to take care of her. I dropped the kids off at Knowledge's mom house. She had been asking me to bring them by for the last week. With all the mess that had been going on I had gotten sidetracked and forgot all about it.

I didn't put up a fight when she told me not to come back because they were staying the night. They already had clothes there, so I wouldn't have to bring them any.

"What was the deal with ol girl back at the school?" Lauren asked once I had cooled off a little bit.

I bit down on my lip hard when she brought up the incident with Jade. No matter how much I told myself I didn't care about Knowledge having yet another child, I did. He had me out here looking like a fool while his side bitch was smiling in my face.

"That bitch used to be one of my close friends until I found out a few days ago that her daughter is Knowledge's." It hurt like hell to admit that to someone I had just met.

"Oh my," was all Lauren could say. But what else could she have said.

"You don't have to keep quiet. If you have something to say, then be my guest and say it," I said. I liked for people to be themselves around me. I wasn't with the putting on a show and faking that I was anything but me. I wanted her to be comfortable enough with me so that I could feel her out a little.

"And you and Knowledge are still together?" she asked.

"I'm done with his ass," I replied, well that's what my mouth was saying. My heart was saying something totally different. A part of me felt like me and Knowledge had put in too many years to just throw everything down the drain. We both had done each other wrong and took each other back every time. But I was sick and tired of the fussing, the fighting, and the cheating. It was time for me to stand my ground. If he wanted my love, he would have to prove to me that he was worthy enough for it.

"No, you're not," she said just as calm.

"What makes you so sure?" I asked.

"Because I was once that girl who couldn't let go of a cheating man that didn't deserve my love. Now by no means am I here to judge you, but I'm a firm believer in once a cheater always a cheater. And even if you do get back with him, you'll always be reminded of all the times that he cheated. Now as for the kid's part, that's the most disrespectful thing you can do in a relationship, next to giving someone a STD. That tells me that you didn't even have the decency to wrap it up. He wasn't thinking about ya health when he was rawing bitches."

I was starting to like Lauren. I could tell she had a lot of hood in her. I couldn't disagree with a thing she was saying because she was right. I needed to let Knowledge be the dog that he was destined to be.

"I can't dispute it." She had just spoken some real shit. Knowledge was a great father and he had a good soul, but when it came to relationships and being faithful, well his ass wasn't shit. "Are you in a rush to get back to the house with Juju?"

"Girl no. You seem like you a real ass female and it's been a long time since I had a female associate I could click with."

"The feeling is mutual."

I drove to my old hood in search of some of my homeboys. You see Jade didn't know I was really about that life for real. I knew with Jade not being able to work at the club she would be selling her pussy left and right, so I wasn't the least bit surprised when I came across her profile online. She was listed on all types of dating sites. Once I found the ones I was looking for, I put them up on game about what had went down. They weren't too pleased about the shit and wanted to go beat her and Knowledge's ass. I gave my number to Toxic and told him to let me know when everything was about to go down. When things were all said and done, Jade thought she would be meeting up with my homeboys for sex, not knowing it would be a setup for her to get her ass whipped. I was hoping they fucked her before I got there.

"How much do I owe you all?" I asked. Nothing in life was free and somebody always wanted something.

"Sanai baby, don't do that. You know it's nothing but love when it comes to you. Even though you won't fuck with the kid," he said putting on his sad puppy dog face. Toxic was a real cool dude. If I needed a situation handled, he was the person I would go see.

Back in the day, Toxic and Knowledge had a slight beef over me. The reason I said slight was because I didn't want him. At the time, I only had my eyes on Knowledge and I wasn't thinking about anybody else. Whenever

Toxic got a chance to do anything for me, he went well out of his way.

"You know I got nothing but love for you." Which was true, I loved Toxic in the sense of an older brother. Nothing more and nothing less. When his phone buzzed, I knew it was nobody but Jade. She was greedy when it came to money. She would've probably given up the nookie for free if she wasn't so hard up on dough. When he was finished confirming everything with Jade, he looked at me with a shady look on his face.

"Man, that girl is down for anything as long as the paper is right."

"Too bad it'll never grease the palms of her hands." I couldn't wait for things to jump off later tonight. Jade was being petty not knowing I was the queen of petty. It was funny how a bitch could fuck ya man and then find a reason to hate you. The things hoes did these days tripped me out.

"Did I take too long?" I said to Lauren as I got behind the wheel. I didn't even notice that she was on the phone.

"You're fine, I was checking up on Juju. From the sound of things, him and Knowledge out handling business."

"I know all about that," I said as I started up the truck. "Since I know that he's not at the house, I can start packing."

"Packing? You going on a trip or something?" Lauren asked.

"I wish, but I sure could use one though. It's been a minute since I've had some time to myself. But nah, Knowledge thought I was playing when I told him not to bring his ass home, so his shit will be outside waiting for him."

"I feel you on that. I have nothing against Knowledge, but I'll be more than happy to help you. I can't stand a no-good ass nigga."

"You sure we haven't met before," I laughed. Something about her was real familiar. I didn't know if we'd crossed paths before or what.

"Not that I can recall."

Before I headed back to the house I stopped at the hardware store. Changing all the locks that Knowledge had keys to was first on my list. One way or another he would get that things were over between us. Around the time the house was built Knowledge had no legal money, so everything was put in my name. The cars and the house. Now I could've cared less about the cars, my only concern was making sure our kids had a place to call home. Knowledge had plenty of money stashed away in those oversea accounts, so it should've been no problem with him giving up the house. I knew Knowledge would put up a fight, and I was willing to go to war. It was the least he could've given me after all the bullshit he had put me through.

With Lauren's help it didn't take me long to box up Knowledge's belongings. I smiled as I placed the last box on the front lawn. It was on him if he didn't get his stuff tonight, or it would be some homeless person's lucky day.

"You were dead serious when you said you were packing up his stuff." Lauren looked around in disbelief. Knowledge had so much stuff he could've given away to about fifty needy people, and still have stuff left over.

"I don't play no games," I replied. For some reason Lauren was growing on me quite a bit. I wasn't about to trust her just yet. Hell, I had only met her a few hours ago. "Are you and Juju together?" I asked being nosey. I loved Juju as if we were birthed from the same mother. I needed to know exactly what Lauren's intentions were. The last bitch had betrayed him, and I refused to let that happen again.

"I don't really know what to call it," she admitted. "Since the day I discovered that he was still alive I felt some type of connection with him. It didn't matter to me that he had money, or that his status was heavy in the streets, I saw so much more in him. I've never in my life met a man that's so sophisticated. I'm not gonna front though, when I read over his charts I thought man he ain't nothing but a thug that sells drugs, but he was so much more than that." I could feel where Lauren was coming from. Knowledge had captured my heart the same way Juju had done hers. It was something about those Santana boys. There was no denying they were some smooth talking, money getting boys.

"All I ask is that you do right by my brother. The last bitch he gave his heart to wasn't shit. She played him and left him for dead. Now I like you and all, but I don't play when it comes to the ones that I love."

"You don't have to worry about that. I'm not the one to play with people's hearts. I done had mine played with several times, and it's not a good feeling."

"I'm glad we have an understanding."

I went in the house and prepared us a quick meal. I needed all my energy when I got the call saying it was time to go to work. Lauren washed the dishes while I swept the floors and cleaned off the table. I couldn't wait to introduce her to Paris. I was sure those two would get along great. After everything was cleaned, I went and changed into some comfortable clothes. Tight as my jeans were, I would not be able to move around like I wanted. Now the waiting game had begun.

Chapter Nine

Knowledge

I was tired of sitting in the truck scoping out the scene at Trina's, while Juju was planning things out. I was ready to put in some work. It would've been nothing for me to go in the house and blow her head off. I hated the bitch and I was mad that Juju was still letting her breathe. I sparked a blunt to calm my nerves. Juju looked at me with a displeased look, but I didn't give a damn. I was grown and if I wanted to smoke some trees then that's exactly what I was going to do.

"You need to be focused when you on these types of jobs," Juju said as he reached over to take the blunt out of my hand. I knew then that he was tripping. Weed never caused me to fall off my game. If anything, it helped me to concentrate better.

"I got this shit over here. You just let me know when it's time to go kick this bitch's door in." I wasn't about to hide my disrespect for Trina. Juju knew exactly how I felt about her.

"Be patient young grasshopper." I took another puff from my blunt. Juju was trying to be funny and I wasn't feeling the shit.

"I've been more than patient. I'm waiting on you to get on ya shit. We been out here long enough to know that the bitch is home alone." If Juju didn't have his mind made up in the next thirty minutes I was pulling off and going to the nearest bodega. A nigga was hungry as hell and my smoke stash was running low.

"You know what? I'm getting real tired of ya mouth. Since you so anxious to put in some work, let's make this shit do what it do." Juju jumped out the car, leaving me to catch up. I put out the blunt and followed suit. By the time I reached the stoop, Juju had already kicked the front door in. Trina looked like she was about to shit a brick when she saw Juju.

"Trick or treat bitch," Juju said as he walked up on her. Trina backed into the corner of the wall, scared to death. She didn't say a word as Juju got even closer to her. "I bet you thought you would never see my face again," Juju grabbed the bottom of her face and squeezed it tightly. I was surprised at how roughly he was handling her. Juju had talked a lot of shit in the car, but I could tell that Trina wouldn't make it to see tomorrow. If she did, that meant he had something real special in store for her.

"I missed you so much," Trina lied. She didn't miss a thing about Juju. She had been spending his money on the next nigga left and right. Juju was the last thing on her mind, and she knew it. I slapped the bitch with my gun, just for talking stupid out of her mouth. I would rather she keep her mouth shut than to say some bullshit like that.
Juju didn't say a word; he knew how I felt about her.

"You lying bitch," Juju spazzed out on Trina. He took his belt off and whooped her ass like she was a child. Trina cried out from the pain she was experiencing. I didn't feel sorry for her conniving ass; she deserved every bit of it.

"Bitch, you left me for dead and you got the fucking nerve to say you've missed me when you done had these niggas all through the house that I paid for. Ya trifling ass even got him wearing my damn chain."

"Juju, you know I would never do anything like that. All these years I've been trying to help Knowledge find out who did this to you." That was it. That bitch had tried it with that lie. Before I could pull my gun back out to send a bullet through her head, Juju had his hands wrapped around her neck.

"I will kill you before you think you're going to sit here and lie in my fucking face." Spit flew out of Juju's mouth as he squeezed her throat even tighter. "I've been watching ya stupid ass for the last year. I know all about the shit you been doing. Either come clean or be prepared to meet the Grim Reaper.

He held her up in the air by her throat, letting her life slip away. Juju slung her down on the floor before she could take her last breath. "If you weren't the bitch that birthed my kids I would let Knowledge go head and get rid of you." Trina coughed up some blood on the carpet. She was trying hard to catch her breath. Juju was putting on a front. The only reason he didn't kill Trina was because he was hurt. He had loved the hell out of Trina, not giving a fuck about anyone else's opinion about her.

"Tell me what you want me to do, I'll do anything. I'll even give you the names of the niggas who set everything up."

"You were going to do that anyway," Juju said. "Don't say a word to anyone about me being alive or else I won't hesitate to come back and split ya wig. You got it?" She nodded her head in agreement, afraid to say too much.

"Where's your phone?" I asked.

She looked at me and rolled her eyes. I don't think she really knew how close to death she was. I wasn't Juju and I had no probably killing her ass.

"Where the fuck is ya phone?" I asked again, only this time my gun was pressed against her temple. I pulled the safety back to let her know I meant business.

"Over there on the chair."

I grabbed her phone and reset the entire thing back to its original settings. That way when we left she wouldn't have access to warn them niggas about us coming. Trina went on and gave up the names and addresses of the niggas that were involved with the robbery to Juju.

Before walking out the door, Juju fired a shot close to hear head in the wall to show her that this shit wasn't a game. That night we went and lit the city up. We made sure to make examples out of anybody that were associated with them niggas. Of course, nobody knew that Juju was behind the shit, but soon enough they would find out. Trina thought she was off limits, but she had another thing coming. When Juju got straight, the first thing he planned on doing was taking his kids and then offing her. That bitch could barely take care of herself, let alone some kids.

♥♥♥♥♥♥

My head was all fucked up when I returned to the house. Sanai had my shit sitting on the lawn like she was having a yard sale. I went to unlock the door, only my key wouldn't turn.

"Fuck!" I screamed out, I couldn't believe this shit. Sanai was still pissed about the stuff with Jade and she had taken things to an entirely different level. All the times we were on the outs she had never pulled no shit like this. I went around to the back door to try my house key, and sure enough, she had changed the locks on that too. I called her phone and she must've hit the ignore button because it went straight to voicemail.

"You good bro?"

"Hell no!" I responded. "Sanai done changed all the fucking locks on the doors. You see she got all my shit out here. I swear I'ma fuck her ass up when I see her."

"Now that's what you're not going to do." Juju jumped to take Sanai's side like he used to always do. "If you would learn to stop fucking with these bitches then you wouldn't be in situations like this." Juju was right, but I wasn't about to agree with him. I tried calling her phone and again I was sent straight to the voicemail.

"Man whatever. You got a place for me to rest at? I'll get a room in the morning. Right now, I don't even feel like dealing with this shit." I walked off and got back in the truck.

"What you gonna do about your stuff?"

"Fuck that shit, I'll buy all new stuff. This ain't nothing to a nigga with money." Sanai was tripping over this Jade shit when we didn't even know if Asia was my daughter. It didn't mean a thing because she looked like our daughter Justice. A baby began to look like any nigga that fed them all the time. Jade was trying to pin her daughter on me when I'm more than sure I wasn't the only nigga that was hitting it. I called Sanai's phone one last time and left a nasty message.

"I see you want to play games and that's cool. I'll give you ya space until you get ya act together. You acting like this the first time we done been through some shit like this. I'm sorry, I know I fucked up, but we can work through this. You already know home is where I want to be. With you and the kids. Don't let a thirsty bitch like Jade fuck up what we have. I love you Jade. Hit me up when you cool off," I sounded like a bitch leaving that message, but I didn't care. I was willing to do whatever it took to get my family back.

Juju drove to this small community out in the suburbs. They had the whole white picket fence thing going on. The lawns were mowed to perfection and expensive cars sat in each of the driveways. I could tell the people out here were living the good life. I watched Juju as he got out the truck to cut off the alarm system. "I'll bring you a blanket and pillow if you plan on sleeping out here in the truck."

"I'll go get a room before I sleep outdoors."

"Then why you still in the truck. Bring ya ass."

Juju gave me a tour of the house before he showed me where I would be staying for the time being. I had to give him his props, it was a nice house. Juju had changed the subject and was talking business, only my mind wasn't focused. The only part of the conversation I caught was that we would be flying out of town next week, which was cool with me. I could use some time to figure this shit out with Sanai.

"I need you to be on your shit. No half-stepping nigga, bring ya A-game," Juju said to me.

"I'm on it," I said to him.

"Well make yaself at home. You know where the kitchen is and ya bathroom is down the hall." I waited until Juju was gone and pulled out my phone.

Babe:

You ain't have to sit my shit outside like that, but I

ain't mad at you. Tell my kids I love them, and I love you too.

I plugged my phone into the wall and sat it down on the nightstand. I grabbed my hygiene products before walking down the hallway into the bathroom. I took a quick shower and dried off. My phone vibrated on the stand. Sanai had replied with the middle finger sign. I laughed at the shit and sent her one back. I was just glad to have heard from her. I laid back on the bed and massaged my dick. A nigga was feeling horny as fuck. I thought about calling Raven and telling her to slide through, but decided against it. The way she ran her mouth the shit would've been back to Sanai within the next hour. Raven couldn't stand Sanai so the first chance she got, she would've threw it in her face. I put Sanai to the back of my head for a moment as I thought about the power move Juju and I were about to make. I was ready to get this money and then I planned on chilling out. If Sanai took me back, I planned on marrying her ass and making up for all the wrong I had done in the past. As far as Jade went, fuck that bitch. She brought all this shit on herself. She knew I was in a relationship with Sanai when she raped me. I didn't give a damn what nobody said. I was drunk, and Jade had taken advantage of me, therefore it was rape. I sparked a blunt while flipping through the channels. I watched a few old episodes of *The First 48*. I couldn't understand how niggas didn't know how to get away with murder. This show showed you how niggas always fucked up. That's why I always said, if you gonna do dirt, do it by yaself. I faced a few more blunts before carrying my ass to bed. A nigga was muthafucking tired.

♥♥♥♥♥♥

My sleep was just getting good when Juju came banging on the door. For the first five minutes I continued to lay there, but the banging only got louder. Juju knew I was a nasty person when I didn't get all my sleep.

"Fuck wrong with you?" I swung the door all the way open and Juju was standing there holding up a black Armani suit with a pair of black Armani dress shoes to match.

"Go get dressed; we got business to take care of. I'll be outside in the limousine waiting for ya ass." It was ten o'clock at night and we were going to a meeting. This was some new shit for me.

We pulled up in the parking lot of a building that was surrounded by people waiting to get inside. Everyone was dressed in their finest attire. The women had on long gowns that dragged across the ground, while the men had on designer suits and flashy jewelry to assemble it all. Juju handed me a ticket with my name and a table number on it.

"What's all this?" I asked. I needed to know what I was getting myself into before walking into something without any clue. I needed to be prepared just in case some shit went down.

"This is the beginning of new things," he said as he got out the car. When we reached the door, I gave the usher my ticket and made my way inside. I stepped inside realizing we were at some type of ball. I felt a little out of place being surrounded by a bunch of foreigners and white people. I wasn't racist or anything, but I just didn't feel comfortable. Juju crept up behind me carrying a glass of champagne in his hand. I gulped the drink down in one swallow. I was gonna need it to get through the night. "Drink, but don't get drunk. When dealing with these types of people things can turn deadly in a matter of seconds." As soon a Juju said that I heard three shots go off before I saw a body hit the ground. Five big African men emerged from out of nowhere to dispose of the body. I ain't gonna lie, it fucked my head up. People were socializing like the shit never happened. Not one person stopped what they were doing to see what was going on. The waitress walked by and I downed another drink. I was way in over my head with this one.

"You weren't playing when you said you had ventured on to some next level shit," I said as I pulled on my goatee. I was trying to figure out where I fit into the mix of all these people. I was ready to see what kind of numbers they were talking.

"Follow me and remain cool. Only speak when spoken to. These are the type of people that will kill you and then feed your body to their pet animals." I didn't like how Juju was talking to me, but I understood where he was coming from. I wasn't trying to put either of us in a situation to be killed over my ignorance.

"No problem boss," I said sarcastically. We both approached a table with a bunch of African looking men. I could tell they stayed ready for war. Down on the floor sat a couple of machetes and a few other swords. I was peeping everything out.

"Julius, nice to see you. Is it about that time again?" For this man to have been calling Juju by his government name, I knew shit had to be the real deal. "Mohamed," Juju said as they both shook hands. "This right here is my brother Knowledge. The one I've been telling you about."

"Nice to meet you," he said, extending his hand out to mine.

"The pleasure is all mine." I could see Juju looking at me from out the corner of his eye. He was probably praying in his head that I didn't say the wrong thing.

"The both of you have a seat," Mohamed said as he motioned for two of his goons to remove their bodies from out of the chairs. He reached down under his seat and pulled out a bag full of the shiniest diamonds I'd ever seen.

"These here are blood diamonds; they come from my country Sierra Leone. I take it that you've heard of it," he said as he examined the diamonds with a magnifying glass.

"I know a little something."

"Good, it's really not much you need to know. I'll supply you with the diamonds, how you distribute them is your business. Your brother here has spoken very highly of you. I only hope that you won't disappoint."

"The auction will be starting in ten minutes." I looked to the stage and that's when I saw the most beautiful woman I had ever seen in my life. Her bronze colored skin was flawless. She stood at about 5'6 with long wavy black hair that hung down to the middle of her back. It was easy to tell that she was of India descent. The sequin gown that she had on hugged every curve on her body. She was a blessing in every man's eyes.

"I see Adhira has captured your attention as well as every other man in this room. Don't be fooled by her beauty, she's the most dangerous woman you'll ever meet. Her looks alone have killed plenty of men."

"I was just admiring her beauty, that's all," I said with my eyes still glued on her. I shook the thoughts of her out of my head. I had enough drama going on with women and I didn't need anymore.

"When and how will I receive the goods?" I was ready to get to the money. With all the people that Juju was affiliated with, I knew it would've been hard to move those diamonds. I just needed to get in with the right people.

Mohamed gave Juju a strange look. "I see you haven't given him a complete rundown on how I conduct business," he said.

"I told him what I felt he needed to know for the time being. I wanted you to feel him out a little before we decided to take this to the next level."

"Good thinking." The serious look Mohamed had been wearing since he'd begun talking had been replaced with a smile. "That alone is why I do business with you. You, unlike a lot of people I've dealt with, think before making a decision that could cost you your life." He waved the waitress over and asked for a few menus. He instructed us to order whatever we liked as he continued to talk.

"Any advice that your brother may give you be sure to listen. He's a very wise man." I nodded my head in agreement. Listening to Juju had kept me off the police's radar on the streets. A few of my homeboys were locked up all because they wanted to be hotheads thinking they knew the game. So, anything that Juju threw my way, I made sure to grasp ahold of it.

"No doubt."

"Come sometime in the next few days you'll be flying out to my country. I want you to see firsthand just what you're getting yourself involved in. Many people have been slaughtered playing in this field. These diamonds right here hold the lives of many families. Once I've determined that you're built for this then you will receive your first shipment through the mail. While my product is in your hands, you will be watched at all times.

I need to be certain that you are loyal. Any signs of deceit, then your family will be mourning your death."

My jaw tightened up a little. I didn't like the way he was talking to me, like I was some kind of whore. The threatening shit was unnecessary, but I understood that this was business. You had to get your point across some way.

"Any questions?"

"None at all."

"Good, you'll receive your plane tickets, along with where you'll be staying before you leave tonight. Now eat up and enjoy the festivities of tonight."

The same woman from earlier appeared back on the stage, only this time she had a heap of exotic looking women with her. Each woman was auctioned off to the highest bidder. A portion of the money was used to help the less fortunate families back in Africa. While the other half went towards the funding of the diamonds. Mohamed paid a hefty price to keep them in stock. The demand for those specific diamonds was high and he refused to lose out on money by not having them. We stayed at the function until it was over.

When we left, I walked out the place with twenty thousand dollars in my pockets. I thought it was some type of advancement until he told me not to worry about paying him back. Right then I knew this nigga was getting serious dough. Nobody just gave away that kind of money without expecting something in return. I tried to give it back until Juju informed me that he gave all his potential clients 'gifts' to see how they would take it. He wanted to see just how greedy people were once they received that type of money in their hands.

To me it wasn't much; I had plenty of money in several bank accounts. I planned on flipping the money he gave me and giving it back to him in triple the amount. Once Mohamed and Juju were finished talking, we went back to the crib where I passed out. I still needed the rest Juju had deprived me of earlier.

Chapter Ten

Sanai

I stood outside the door of the room that Jade and Toxic were in. I could hear the loud moans coming from the both of them, so I knew they were deep into it. Lauren was by my side ready for whatever that was about to go down. I didn't want her tagging along, but she insisted on coming.

I didn't know if she felt obligated to look after me because I considered Juju my brother or what. Silently I slid the spare key card into the slot. Once the light turned green I barged into the room and went to work. I snatched Jade from off the bed by her hair and delivered punches to her face unmercifully. I released every bit of anger I had built up inside of me on her ass. I was tired of her steady fucking with me when I hadn't done a damn thing to her in the first place.

Toxic was in the corner laughing his ass off as he put on his clothes. He retrieved his money from off the nightstand and bounced. With each blow I delivered I made sure to talk to her.

"I'm fucking sick of you! Its bitches like you who make it hard for women like me," I said quoting Lisa Raye from the movie *Player's Club*. Jade didn't have a real reason as to why she disliked me. She was just jealous. See these bitches wanted everything you had until they got it and saw the shit that came along with it. She didn't really want Knowledge; she wanted the happiness she thought I had. Even with a bloody mouth, she still managed to talk shit.

"If I can get a reaction out of you like this then I'm still on top of my shit." Somehow, she managed to use her weight and get me off her. She got a few good licks in before Lauren pulled her ass back down to the ground. I swear if I wasn't so afraid of my children going into foster care I would've killed that bitch. I was starting to see that I wouldn't have peace in my life until she was gone for good.

"Stay the hell away from me and my kids. As far as Knowledge, you can have him. You two dirty bitches deserve each other." I kicked her all over her body until I felt a set of hands trying to pull me away from her. Toxic had come back just in time. A minute later and Jade would've been dead. The thoughts of her having a baby by Knowledge crossed my mind. I kicked her dead in her pussy for the hell of it. I didn't care if the bitch never carried another baby a day in her life. She wasn't worthy of being someone's mother.

"Let's get out of here," Lauren said as she looked out the door to make sure the coast was clear. For a second I thought about taking her car keys and making her find a way home, but I wasn't that petty. I had only come here to show her what happened when you decided to play with my kids. She was lucky I didn't do as much damage as I wanted to.

"Take the stairs, your car is waiting for you out back," Toxic said. I asked no questions as I wondered how the hell he moved my car when the keys were in my pocket. But then I remembered I was dealing with a nigga straight from the hood. They had ways of making anything possible. By the time I made it to the bottom step, I was out of breath. I needed to get back in shape if I planned on giving out ass whippings on a regular. I was thankful when Lauren jumped into the driver's seat. My wrist thumped terribly. I figured I had sprained it when I fell on my hand. When I got to the house the first thing I did was crush up a bag of ice with the one free hand I

could use. I placed a towel over the ice and let it rest there until my hand became numb. I popped a Tylenol to help ease some of the pain.

"I didn't think you could throw hands like that," Lauren admitted.

"What would make you think something like that?"

"Because most pretty girls can't fight," she said being honest. I didn't know whether to take it as a compliment or an insult, so I responded with a simple 'Thank you'. I had a few messages come through on my phone from Knowledge. I deleted it without bothering to see what it said. Right now, I wasn't feeling him at all. I was starting to believe that there was no hope in saving our relationship. He had betrayed the little trust I had left in him. It no longer mattered about how much I loved him, if I couldn't trust him, there was no way we could be together. We probably would've worked things out like the rest of the times had it been somebody I didn't know.

But nah, it had to be a bitch I had known for years. Someone I had once considered a friend. Out of all the bitches in Brooklyn, he had to bring the shit so close to home.

With the extra time I had on my hands, I planned on mending my relationship with my mother. It had been years since we'd spoken, and it was time to change that. Regardless of what we couldn't agree on, she was still my mother, and at the end of the day I only got one. I only hoped it wasn't too late.

"You can stay in one of the extra bedrooms upstairs if you don't feel like driving home this late."

"Thanks for the invitation because I am tired. I don't think I can make it home without falling asleep behind the wheel." I told her where everything she needed was located before calling it a night. My body needed to rest. I was so tired I didn't even make it to the bathroom to take a shower.

♥♥♥♥♥♥

When I woke up the next day it was already one o'clock in the afternoon. I rolled over and checked my phone to see if I had any missed calls and sure enough, I had several. Knowledge's mother sent me a text saying she planned on keeping the kids for a few more days. A part of me wanted to tell her that they had to come home. I missed the sounds of them running around the house and fighting every few minutes. I sent her a text back letting her know that it was fine with me. With the kids being gone, it gave me time to get caught up on some work. I had been so occupied with the drama, I had allowed my orders to get backed up and that wasn't something that I did. I grabbed my body wash from off the dresser and ran into the bathroom. I took a quick shower and washed up all the important spots real good. After doing a smell check, I jumped out the shower and threw on some lounging clothes. Today was one of those days when I didn't plan on leaving the house unless it was an emergency. I had work to do.

I grabbed my laptop and walked down the stairs when I ran into Lauren carrying a tray of food.

"Good morning, or should I say good afternoon."

"You just don't know how bad I needed that sleep," I said. I had forgotten all about her being at the house.

"All of this is for you." She walked back down the stairs and sat the tray down on the ottoman. Eating was the last thing on my mind as I jumped into my work. I wanted to kick myself in the ass once I saw how many orders needed to be completed. Well over a hundred waist trainers needed to be shipped off before the next morning. Lauren didn't know it yet, but I planned on putting her ass to work as well.

"You work today?" I asked.

"Not that I know of. While I was taking care of Juju I changed my status to on call, so they only call me when they need me, and even then, I decide whether or not I want to go in." *Perfect,* I thought to myself.

"Well if you don't have any other plans, I could really use your help with these orders."

"Okay sure. But what type of orders are we talking about?" I went ahead and told her about the business that I owned. She seemed to be a little impressed. I got the feeling she thought I was the type of chick to sit around and wait on a nigga to take care of me. Even if she didn't, I felt the need to make it clear anyway. I went ahead and showed her how to read the orders. Two hours had passed, and we had knocked out half of the orders. I stopped what I was doing when I heard the doorbell ring.

"Let it ring. People know better than to come to my house before checking first." I wasn't in the mood to have company. Paris was still in the hospital, so I had no clue as to who it could've been.

"You sure you don't want me to get it?" Whoever was at the door was determined to get a response. I cursed when I looked through the peephole to see that Juju was the one making all the noise. Of course, Knowledge was right beside him. I walked back into the living room and took a seat. If Lauren wanted to answer the door then it was on her.

"Where them niggas at?" Juju said half-jokingly as he hugged me.

"If I had a nigga up in here then he would either be in one or two places; my bed or between my legs," I said with a smirk on my face.

"Lil sis don't play. I'll kill everything moving around here." Knowledge stood against the wall with his hands in pockets, looking stupid in the face. I had no words for him, so I didn't know why he was even here.

"I know you will bro."

"I take it that you two get along with no problems," Juju said referring to me and Lauren. He knew I didn't do the whole mingling with female's thing.

"Yeah, she cool as shit. I think you got a keeper on the team," I said putting in a good word for Lauren. I turned my back so that Juju couldn't see me and winked my eye at Lauren who was in the kitchen cleaning up.

"We'll see how things go. I'm not trying to put my all into another female," Juju said in a whisper.

"You can't compare her to Trina. We all tried to warn you about that bitch." Juju knew there were no cut cards with me. I said how I felt at all times. Sometimes I was a little too blunt, but that was just me.

When Laruen came back into the living room, I gave them their privacy and went upstairs. I was more than sure Knowledge would find his way sniffing up my ass. I prepared myself for whatever bullshit he was about to say out of his mouth.

"Can we talk for a minute?" Knowledge entered the room and sat down on the bed. He only had a minute, so I didn't know why he was making himself so comfortable.

"Ya minute has already started, so talk."

"I know things ain't always been the best between us, but I know we can work through this. Even if you don't believe it, Jade really did rape me. I'ma keep it a buck with you, I did double back a few times, but it meant nothing. Now as far as Asia is concerned, I ain't seen no papers stating that she is mine."

I guess Knowledge called himself coming cleaning, but it was too late. For two years he played me like a fool. He was going around pumping babies inside of every hoe around town like he was exempt from catching HIV or AIDS. I was glad I got tested on the regular. Knowledge was hazardous to my health as well as his own. With all the men Jade messed around with it was no telling what she had.

"Do you really expect me to believe that Asia isn't yours? Even Stevie Wonder can see that she's yours." I had to walk out the room for a minute to prevent Knowledge from seeing the tears that threatened to surface.

There was a time in life where I would've rode for this man. Right hand on the bible I would've lied and did his time if it came down to it. I know it probably sounded crazy but that's the type of bitch I was. I was loyal until the end. When I was with a person I put my all into them. My world literally revolved around them and everything they did. I put my own happiness on the back burner while I pleased a muthafucka that really didn't give a damn about it. His words may have said one thing, but his actions spoke another. I walked back into the room and stood directly in front of Knowledge. I wanted him to see every emotion that I held in my face.

With all my might I drew my hand back and smacked fire out of his ass. Instead of getting mad like I thought he would, he pulled me down onto the bed and wrapped his legs around me. Knowledge planted small kisses on the nape of my neck. He knew that shit would drive me crazy. I tried to push away from him, but with each kiss he made my body grow weak.

"What are you doing Knowledge?" I asked him as a few moans accidently escaped my mouth.

"Don't fight it. You know you want it just as bad as I do," he whispered into my ear. Knowledge was a smooth talker. He knew all the right things to say to get inside of your pants. I had a trick for him though. I was gonna get my nut and leave him feeling like a trick.

My body shivered when I felt him place two of his fingers inside of me. I threw my hips forward as he worked them in and out. It wasn't long before my pussy juices were dripping all over his hands. I was tired of the role play; I was ready to get down to the real things.

"Put it in," I moaned as he rubbed on my clit. He rubbed his dick up and down my opening, until I stopped him. "Grab a condom from out the drawer," I said to him. I knew all about the secret stash he kept beside the bed. He mumbled something smart underneath his breath, but he still put it on. I gasped when he entered me. Knowledge had been blessed well between his legs. He slow stroked me at first until he saw that I wasn't moaning. I bit down on my lip so that I couldn't make a sound.

"You know you love this dick." With each pump Knowledge gave, my pussy got wetter. He wasn't lying either. Knowledge had that dope dick, which was probably why I was so stupid over him. He had a way of pleasing your body like no other man. My clit throbbed as I released my cream all over his dick.

"I got mine; now get up off me." He acted like he wasn't comprehending what I said until my fist landed up against his head. His ass got the point then. I went in to the bathroom and cleaned the musty smell of sex from off me. Knowledge had just got played at his own game. Since he like to play games, I planned to mess with his head. I walked out the bathroom and changed into some real clothes. I was ready to get out of the house and away from him.

"That was real fucked up." I looked at this nigga like he had a lot of nerve. I told myself I was done letting him get the best of me, but I lied. I went in on all his without pulling off. He was in his feelings about some pussy, but he didn't give a damn about my feelings when he was hiding a baby.

"No what's fucked up is how I had ya back all these years and you treated me like shit. What's fucked up is how I thought you had changed. What's fucked up is how you love making extra mouths to feed when you barely spend time with the kids that we have together. So, don't sit there and come at me sideways cause you didn't get ya nut."

"I'm out of here. I ain't got to listen to this shit."

"Then get the fuck out then nigga. I don't know why you brought ya ass here in the first place. Now, we can still do business together if you choose. I'm not that petty to mess over your money, especially when I have my own." I threw that out there just to remind Knowledge that I didn't need him, which he knew. His dick might've been good, but it wasn't that good to where I would allow him to continue to disrespect me. I was officially fed up with his shit. He needed to feel the same pain that he had caused me. I wasn't being mean, but I was on some get back shit.

Chapter Eleven

Paris

The day had finally come when I would be released from this hospital. I had been in here for almost a month, and I was ready to go. After weeks of physical therapy, I was finally up and moving on my own. Of course, I still got some pain here and there, but it wasn't much.

I looked into the mirror as I applied my makeup. Sanai had come through for me earlier and hooked my hair up. I was surprised to see she had a female with her, which I'd never seen before. I knew how Sanai was about interacting with new people. Nonetheless she seemed cool and down to earth. As long as she was nothing like Jade, then she was fine with me. If Sanai could get along with her then she had to be alright. I applied a golden eyeshadow to my lids and was satisfied with the way I looked.

I ignored my phone as it rang. My mother had been calling me since first thing this morning wanting to know when I was on my way. She was determined that I would be staying with her until I got on my feet, but that wouldn't be the case. I loved my mom, but I couldn't be around her every single day. We were both too much alike. It wouldn't be long before the both of us caught an attitude and then she would be threatening to put me out. So, to avoid all of that, Romeo had volunteered his place and I took him up on his offer. We had both agreed that this didn't change our status and that we would remain friends until we felt that we were ready to move things to the next level.

"You ready to go ma?" Romeo greeted me with a passionate kiss on my lips, which caught me off guard. I was so use to the small specks that he gave me; I never saw that one coming.

"I'm just waiting on them to bring my release papers and prescriptions."

"I'll go ahead and take your stuff down to the car then."

While Romeo was gone the nurse came in with the instructions and the take it easy speech. I was told to do no heavy lifting and all the basic stuff. I signed the paper on the clipboard, grabbed my purse from off the bed, and went to find Romeo.

The ride over to Romeo's was quiet. I was deep in my thoughts about the new life I planned on living. Legend was now a thing of the past, but I couldn't shake the feeling I got when I thought about Jade. I had really considered her to be a friend and it hurt me to think about how she betrayed me. I was the one who always looked out for her when everyone was against her, including her own sister. I turned the radio on to take my mind off her. When I heard Jazmine Sullivan's "Let it Burn" on the radio my mood changed instantly. Her voice was so powerful. There wasn't a song that she had that I couldn't relate to. This song described how I felt about

Romeo, only I hadn't told him yet. I turned the volume up on the radio and sang along with her not missing a beat.

Feel it creepin' in your heart

Ooh, baby can you feel it tearing you apart?

That's right that's love

When it comes, you never wanna give it up

And, baby, I'm caught in the light and I ain't gonna fight it

There's no use in tryin', I'm yours

And I want you to want me the way that I want you and more

(So if you're ready to take this ride

We could go all around the world, baby

Shit, we could even go to the stars if you like)

I know it's scary

'Cause someone always get hurt when you're caring

And I felt that way too

But ready or not, it's coming for you

You feel that fire, just let it burn

There's no runnin' when it's your turn

Call me crazy but I think I found the love of my life

Just let it burn

Let it, let it burn

Just let it burn

Let it, let it burn

Call me crazy but I think I found the love of my life

"So, you found the love your life huh?" Romeo laughed, showing off that smile that made me tingle down below. "You got some vocals on you too baby girl."

"I don't know if it's love that I'm feeling or if it's lust. All I know is that I can't stop thinking about you when I'm away from you. You've sparked something inside of me that I haven't felt in long time. You helped me find myself again."

I had never been one to express my feelings. I normally kept everything bottled up inside of me before I finally exploded. I was attracted to more than just his looks. The more I got to know him, the more I realized that he wasn't just a nigga from the streets; he had the potential to be much more. I felt like we could become a power couple once we both got on the same page and became one. I placed my hands on top of his as he drove up the highway. I fixed my lips to say something, but I became stuck. I gave it one more try before finally blurting out the words "I love you."

"I didn't quite catch that. Can you repeat that for me?"

"Don't play. You heard exactly what I said," I punched him in his arm gently.

"I love you too ma," Romeo said.

I blushed when he said those words back to me. I felt like he really meant what he said. Since day one he had been by my side. He wasn't obligated to do anything for me, but still he chose to.

"I know you don't approve of my dealings in the streets which is why I have a surprise for you. Paris, you ain't like most of the females I've dealt with. There aren't too many that can say they've held my attention as long as you have. Now I'm far from the perfect nigga, but when I see something worth having I try to put my all in it. I just have to know that you're willing to do the same. Have my back the way that I intend on having yours. Respect me and I'll give you the same in return. Be my backbone and in return I'll give you the world that you deserve."

Romeo had me feeling like I was a school girl with her first crush. I didn't even remember my feelings being this strong for Legend when I first met him.

"I'm ready to rock with you the long way," I said.

Romeo pulled into the parking lot of a car dealership which was surrounded by nothing but foreign cars. I felt my heart skip a beat when I saw my dream car was amongst one of them. I took out my phone and snapped a quick picture of the gold Panamera Porsche. I didn't really care too much for the funny shape, but still it was something that I always dreamed of having. The inside was quite remarkable.

"What are we doing here? People are going to call the police on us for trespassing?" I said panicking.

"You can't trespass on your own property."

"What you talking about Romeo?"

"This is the surprise I was talking about in the car. It's been in the making for the last year, only now it's about to be open for the public."

"Romeo stop playing before you mess around and send me back to the hospital for having a heart attack," I said being serious. I thought it was all joke until he pulled the keys out of his pocket and opened the door.

"One thing I don't do is play games ma. I thought back to the night we were having dinner and you told me how you felt about drug dealers. Seeing how much dislike you had for them made me push a little harder. Nobody wants to sell dope forever. So, a few weeks ago I signed the last paper I needed to make this right here official. Everything you see is legit, and it's owned by yours truly." Romeo had me speechless with this one. I didn't think he really cared about my opinion or that he was paying attention.

"Come on, there's something else that I want to show you."

Hand in hand, we walked inside. Romeo gave me a complete tour of the dealership. I had to admit I was impressed with what he had going on. The décor was on point and everything matched to a tee. I didn't think he had this much style in him.

"Go ahead and go in while I run to my office real quick." Romeo took off leaving me standing at the door. I walked in wondering whose office I was in. I could've sworn Romeo said he had to run to his office. The entire office was decorated with the colors pink and black, so it was easy to see it was for a woman, or either a gay man.

"How you feeling about the place?"

"I like it. Everything is real nice."

"What you think about this office?"

"I love the colors."

"I knew you would. I had this office designed for you; I want you to come work for me. Come be a part of the team and join the movement."

"Are you serious? This right here is mine? Why you got to be playing with my emotions like this?" I said.

"How many times are we gonna have to go over this. When I say something, I'm being all the way honest with you. Now either you're gonna say no or I'ma have to hire somebody else."

"Don't play me like that you know the answer is yes."

"Good, I don't plan on opening until you get situated. I don't want you jumping back into the work scene if you aren't ready." I thanked Romeo for the new job. Things were finally looking up for me. I looked around the room, trying to figure out what pictures I planned on hanging up. The office was very spacious, and I had a nice view of the front parking lot. My eyes settled on the car that I was looking at earlier. I didn't care how many hours I had to work, by the end of next year that Porsche was going to be mine.

"What are you looking at?" Rome came up behind me and placed his arms around my waist. I relaxed my body as I leaned back into him. It felt good to be in his muscular arms.

"That gold car out there will be mine. Watch what I tell you."

"You like it that much?"

"Yeah. I've dreamed of owning one ever since I was a little girl. I use to tell my dad I didn't care what color it was as long as I got one."

"Say no more. It's yours." I turned around so that I could see what expression he wore on his face.

"No need to look at me like that. I already told you I plan on giving you the world. If you want it just say the word and there it is." My inner freak was beginning to surface. I got down on my knees and gave him the best head of his life. It was my way of saying thank you until we got to the house.

♥♥♥♥♥♥

Ever since I'd been staying with Romeo we hadn't been doing nothing but engaging in hot sex. Every chance we got we were going at it like dogs in heat. Even though the doctors told me that it was a slim chance of me getting pregnant, I still used birth control as a precaution. A

few nights ago, over a candle dinner, me and Romeo decided to go ahead and make things official between us. I was in the kitchen fixing myself a smoothie when I heard something vibrating. Romeo's phone was going off on the coffee table. I picked his phone up to go take it to him when I saw the name Kemia flash across the screen with a text asking when he was coming through. I didn't need to see anymore. I rushed into the kitchen and grabbed a butcher knife as I went running up the stairs two at a time.

"Who the hell is Kemia?" I said as I went charging at him with the knife.

"What the hell are you talking about Paris?" He didn't even flinch as I pressed the knife against his neck.

"The bitch that's texting ya phone asking when you are coming over," I said pressing the knife further into his skin. I wasn't trying to hurt him; I just wanted him to know that I refused to get played again.

My heart couldn't take any more pain. Love wasn't about to win this time. For all that I would place my heart under lock and key before I allowed another man to break it into a million pieces. With my free hand, I showed him the message, so he could see exactly what I was talking about.

"If you would've read the previous messages you would see that Kemia is the one who twists my dreads." I placed the knife down on the bed and apologized, but he wasn't trying to hear it.

"I'm sorry," I said, rubbing my hands up and down his ribcage.

"It's not gonna work." Romeo pushed my hands away. He went into the closet and came back out with a pair of Timberlands in his hand.

"Where you going?"

"Out for a drink. You got me fucked up with this one. Not once have I given you a reason to question anything that I say. I've kept it a buck with you since I met you and you put a knife to my throat. You got me fucked up. I'm not like that last nigga you were fucking with. So instead of me choking ya dumb ass out right now, I'ma leave and go get my mind right."

"You don't have to leave the house, stay in with me and I'll make it up to you." I couldn't believe I was standing here begging for a man to stay in the house with me. I admit I was wrong for jumping to conclusions and assuming that he was smashing someone else, but what woman wouldn't go off if she'd seen a message from another woman in her man's phone. I jumped up and blocked the door so that he couldn't leave the room.

"Yo, move out the way."

"No! I'm not moving, and you aren't going anywhere."

"Either you move or I'm going to move you myself."

Romeo was going to have to do whatever he saw fit, I was not about to lose my man to another woman. I overreacted when I should've just come to him first. I still had an issue with trusting him completely and I was working on that. I had brought old baggage into a new relationship when I should've just left it in the past. It was hard believing every word someone told you when you had been lied to a thousand times. I couldn't believe I was about to mess things up with the one man who cared about me. No woman wanted to be cheated on so could you blame me for reacting the way that I did?

"You know what, I'ma go ahead and give you ya space," I said and moved away from the door. "But if you do anything to jeopardize what we have, then we're done. I was woman enough to admit my faults, but from here on out it's on you." I was hurt when he walked out the door, not saying a word. I thought he would change his mind and stay in. I looked out the window and watched him pull out the driveway. I picked up my phone and dialed Sanai's number. I wasn't about to sit around and wait on any man. I felt like I needed to get my mind right also.

Chapter Twelve

Romeo

Paris had pissed me off with that dumb shit she pulled back at the house. I had kept it nothing but a buck with her and she felt the need to question some shit she'd seen in my phone. I thought we were way better than that. I wasn't the type of nigga to play games with any bitch, and I could see that Paris would learn that shit the hard way.

It was still early in the night, so I decided to stop by the strip joint before it got too packed. I didn't consider looking at another bitch as cheating since I wasn't engaging in any sexual activity. When I saw how long the line was to get in, I started to turn around, but then I remembered who I was. I walked up to the door, bypassing every one that was waiting to get in. The bouncer immediately dapped me up and let me in.

"What's poppin Romeo?"

"Ain't shit, just trying to see some ass that's all."

"Ain't nothing wrong with it." I slid him a c-note for looking out and went straight to the bar. I was still fucked up in the head about that stunt that Paris had pulled. If shit would've been the opposite of what it was, I would've been laid out on the floor leaking. I laughed when I really thought about the shit. Paris had a little hood in her after all. I knew it would come out eventually. Paris possessed something that a lot of women didn't have nowadays. She carried herself with class, but would show out when she needed to. I don't think Paris realized how much I loved her. She had me going hard for her, and I didn't go hard for no female except my momma and my sister. I wanted to be with her, but she was going to have to cut all that accusing shit out. If I wanted to fuck around with other bitches I would've never committed myself to her.

"Paris done finally let the leash off ya ass." Knowledge had two bad ass females on each of his arms. One of the girls favored Kat Stack's a little bit. Women would forever be his weakness.

"I see you out thotting," I said, dapping him up.

"You got it right. Only thing is I don't love these hoes, I'm just out here to get my dick wet," Knowledge said being honest.

"Nigga ya ass gonna fuck around and catch something that you can't get rid of."

"Ain't nobody trying to hear that shit," Knowledge said brushing me off. A bottle of Henny later, I was turnt all the way up. I sat in front of the stage throwing big bucks at all the girls who danced. It wasn't anything spectacular about the performances. Almost every girl had the same dance routine, or they did the same old moves. Making their ass clap and breaking out into splits.

It was time for them to become original. The strip clubs up north had nothing on the ones I'd been to down in the dirty south. Those bitches down there really knew how to put on a show. I'm talking, picking up beer bottles with their pussies and a whole bunch of other freaky shit.

It was one girl that I had been tipping well all night. She was real thick. She kind of reminded me of Paris, which was probably the reason for her getting most of my money. I had to get away from there before I messed around and spent all the money I had on me.

♥♥♥♥♥♥

Somehow, I had ended up in the VIP section spending more money on the same girl. After a few dances, I found out that her name was Sandra and that she hated dancing. She claimed she was only dancing to pay her tuition for college, but that's what they all said. I didn't know her full story, so I wasn't about to judge her. Not every female that worked in the strip club was a thot. Some did what they had to do to take care of home, while others enjoyed the fast life and the money.

"I got up to leave but she stopped me."

"Please don't go," she begged. "You don't have to spend any more money; I just like your company. I'm not ready to go back out there and deal with all of those thirsty ass men." The liquor had me feeling nice, but I

wasn't drunk. She wasn't about to put me in the trick bag like that. Just minutes ago, she was telling me how bad she needed the money, and now she was saying I didn't have to pay for any dances. She must've thought I was a sucka

ass nigga who didn't know the game. The man standing outside the door didn't care if she said I didn't have to pay, he still wanted his money once I came out. I declined her offer to stay in the politest way possible and got the hell out of there.

I went to the bathroom to drain some of the alcohol out of my system when I spotted Paris at the bar with one of the male strippers smiling all in her face. Paris always had the same expression on her face, so I couldn't tell if she was feeling the nigga or what. I pushed my way through the crowd spilling a few drinks in the process, but I didn't care. A nigga was on a mission to check dude about being in my woman's face. This would be the time for me to check Paris as well while I was at it. She had no business having him in her face in the first place.

"Yo son, you need to back the fuck up."

"You know this clown?" he said to Paris. Before she even had a chance to respond, I grabbed his neck and smashed his head into the counter. He had me confused with another nigga when he said that clown shit out of his mouth. I continued to smash his head until the bouncer had to take me out. But I wasn't leaving without Paris, so just as quickly as they grabbed me; I snatched her ass up too.

"You hurting me," Paris said as I threw her ass into the car. I was tired of playing around with her. She must've not realized that she had a boss nigga by her side. I wasn't one of these lame ass niggas that would put up with her being petty. I would kick her ass to the curb before I sat up here and played these childish mind games with her. She was lucky she was breathing now after

pulling that knife out of me. Had she had been any other bitch I would've smacked her brains loose.

"Am I not good to you?" I asked. I was racing through traffic and running red lights as I did well past ninety trying to get to the house.

"Romeo, slow down before you kill us both."

"You must not know that I will crash this car with the both of us in it." I pushed down harder on the gas pedal. The speedometer was now reading one hundred and ten. I was bluffing. I was only trying to scare her up a little bit. It must've worked because she was over in her seat talking about how she didn't want to die so soon. I almost laughed, until I caught myself.

"Now answer the fucking question. Am I not good to you?"

"Yes," she said in between the tears and sobs.

"Then why would you be so disrespectful and have a nigga in your face?"

"He was asking me what type of perfume I had on because he liked the smell of it and wanted to buy it for his girlfriend."

I could tell she was telling the truth, but I wasn't done with her quite yet. "Yeah, tell me anything that sound good. You must think I'm stupid. I ought to push ya ass out this car right now, while it's moving." When I said

that, she hit the lock button on her door and went to grab the steering wheel. I swerved into the next lane barely missing a tractor trailer that was coming our way. When I regained control of the wheel I hit the brakes real hard, causing her head to fly back and hit the seat. When we got to the house she rushed inside and locked herself in the bathroom.

I heard water running in the bathroom and decided enough was enough. I lit some vanilla scented candles and quickly prepared a tray with some strawberries and whipped cream. I turned on "Sweet Lady" by Tyrese and waited for Paris to exit the bathroom.

Chapter Thirteen

Paris

Sweet lady would you be my

Sweet love for a lifetime

I'll be there when you need me

Just call and receive me

Sweet lady would you be my

Sweet love for a lifetime

I'll be there when you need me

Just call and receive me

I didn't care how many slow jams Romeo played, I wasn't coming out of the bathroom any time soon. I guess you really didn't know a person until they revealed their true colors. It was funny how earlier he was bitchin about me assuming stuff, and here he was doing the same thing. I had every right to be upset. Not even thirty minutes ago he was in the car trying to kill me. It was bad enough he had embarrassed me the way he did at the club. I knew he probably thought I was lying about the perfume answer, but I didn't care. I told him the truth and as far as I was concerned that should've been the end of it.

I took the washcloth and let the hot water run down the sore spots of my body. Romeo had left a few nasty bruises on my arm when he grabbed me. I was starting to believe that I was better off being single. The relationship stuff was starting to be a bit much for me. I wanted to have sex, be happy, and live comfortably while getting the respect that I deserved from the man that I loved.

Romeo didn't have to worry about me seeking comfort in the arms of another man. I knew how it felt to be hurt and that was the last thing I wanted him to feel. He really was a good man, and it had nothing to do with the material things that he provided. I fell in love with him for being there for me when no one else was. He showed me it was possible to love again after being hurt.

Right now, I was just being stubborn. Leaving Romeo was the last thing I planned on doing. I had mixed emotions running through my mind. I didn't know if I should have gone out there and catered to his every need, or if I should've kept up with my attitude and stayed mad. I let the cold water out of the tub and ran some hot water. After scrubbing my body down, I washed all the soap off and applied my nightly facial cream to my face.

I looked in the mirror and what I saw had me all in my feelings. I really needed to get myself together. The scar on the left side of my face reminded me of the fire that Legend had put me through. I felt like I would never get over the pain that he caused me. Because of him I was having a hard time accepting the love that Romeo was trying so hard to give me.

Legend's court date was coming up soon and I wanted to be there when the judge read his fate. I wanted his ass to burn and rot. He had me suffering in hell. He didn't even deserve to breathe the same air as me, let alone walk the grounds of this earth. He was locked away right now, but it wasn't enough. He needed to pay for all the pain he had put me through. I wanted to run away from the all the pain that I was feeling. But there was no escape. I still woke up in the middle of the night with nightmares thinking that he was hiding in my closets or underneath the bed waiting for a chance to attack me. I had even contemplated getting counseling to help me cope with what I'd been through.

I loved Romeo, but I couldn't give him my all because I was afraid of being hurt again. It was no use in receiving love if I couldn't give the same back in return. I had to do something before I lost my mind and Romeo. I was over Legend, yet he was still haunting my soul. When I realized how Romeo treated me compared to Legend, I felt foolish for the way I was acting. Instead of being childish, I should've been ready, willing, and able to accept anything that he brought my way. The man had even opened a dealership to please me. If he could leave the streets alone for me, then there was no reason why I couldn't cooperate with him. I sprayed on some sweet-smelling perfume before I walked out the door to my man.

When I walked into the bedroom, Romeo was laid back on the bed smoking a blunt in nothing but his Polo boxers. My nipples tingled when I saw the imprint of his manhood standing at attention. I wanted to go over there and jump on his dick, but my pride wouldn't allow me to do it. I swore this would be the last time I let Legend interfere with our relationship. After I went to his sentencing, he would no longer exist in my world.

"Quit pouting like a child and get over here," Romeo demanded rather than asking. I walked over to him with my arms folded across my chest and my lips poked out. I wasn't ready to give in just yet.

"I apologize for what went down at the club. I didn't mean to rough ya ass up the way I did. I let my jealousy get the best of me, and I was wrong. Seeing that man in ya face brought back cold memories of my last real relationship. That bitch did some shit that hurt me to my soul."

Normally I would've asked him to go into details, but I didn't. If he told me who the girl was then it would've only caused me to act jealous. I already had self-esteem issues and I didn't need anymore.

"I accept your apology," I said, slowly letting my attitude fade away.

"Do you love me?" he asked. I looked at him funny. If I didn't love him I would be headed to my mother's house with all my belongings in tow.

"Of course, I do."

"Well show a nigga you love him then."

I stood and turned my back towards him while I took off my robe. Even though we'd had sex before, I was still self-conscious about him seeing my body.

"If you don't turn around and face me. I want to see every inch of your body. As long as you're with me you don't have to ever be ashamed of what God has blessed you with. I want you to know that you're a blessing in my eyes." Romeo was going to cause me to cry. I was the one who had started the whole argument and here he was steady giving compliments and making up to me.

I got on my knees and climbed over to Romeo. I stopped once I stood face to face with his pelvic area. I grabbed both of my breasts and licked my nipples in a circular motion. I did this while staring into his eyes. I flicked my tongue back and forth before biting down on them. I released a few moans. I was so caught up in the moment I never even saw when Romeo took off his boxers.

Romeo stroked his dick while I twirled my hips. The sensations that took over my body had me trembling. I crawled over to Romeo and rocked his mic. I took all ten inches down the back of my throat like a pro. I was surprised at myself. I didn't think I had it in me. I spit on his dick to make it real wet before proceeding to lick around his head. I wasn't just sucking his dick, I was making love to it. The more I slurped the louder his moans grew.

"God damn," he hollered out. I knew my head game was official when he grabbed the back of my neck and pushed me down further. That's when I cupped his balls into my hand and got them wet too. I sucked his dick until I saw the veins popping out. I took both of his balls into my mouth and sucked his dick at the same time. I wanted to please Romeo in every way possible, and from the looks of things, I was doing one hell of a job.

"That's enough," he said, catching his breath. His chest heaved up and down. "That shit was straight fire, but now it's my turn. Lay on ya stomach for me." Romeo spread apart both of my ass cheeks before sticking his tongue deep inside my love box.

"Hmmm," I said, throwing my ass back into his face. I gripped the bed sheets to keep from running away. When he sucked on my clit I could feel my juices squirting down on his tongue. Romeo picked up the towel from off the floor to wipe away my juices that were on his face. I held one of my legs up in the air so that he had perfect access to enter my body.

I gasped when I felt his thickness. Romeo started off with a few slow strokes before he picked up the pace. I tried to match my rhythm with his, but there was no way I could keep up with him.

"Shiiitttttt!" I screamed out loud as he went in deeper. He was literally all up in my guts. He played with my pearl and gave a couple more pumps. I could feel my warm juices gushing from out of my pussy. I was so wet his dick fell out a couple of times.

"Go ahead and nut for daddy." When he bit down on my earlobe, I lost it. The sex was so good I had tears coming down my face. I had never experienced that kind of loving before. He took his time with my body, making sure I got mine off before he did. He gave me a high that I

didn't want to come down from. Sex was good for the body, but it was even better for the soul when it was with the person you loved.

"I love you Romeo!" I cried out.

"Ahh, I love you too Paris."

After a few more minutes of him pounding, we both reached our climax. We got up and showered together, right before we fell asleep in each other's arms. I wanted the love I had for this man to last forever. I was finally ready to love again.

Chapter Fourteen

Legend

I woke up this morning feeling like a million bucks. Today I would stand trial for the shit that happened with Paris, but I wasn't sweating it. A nigga knew that he was getting off scot-free. Every time it came time to be evaluated by the doctors, I played crazy to the extreme. Anything that made me look insane, then you best believe I did it.

I hadn't had contact with nobody in the outside world since I'd been in this hell hole. My own father had disowned me. He made it clear that he wasn't coming down here for any visits, or putting any money on my books. I knew I had violated his trust what I harmed Paris. But the shit was done now, and I didn't plan on taking it back either.

I was playing the insane role so well I didn't even bother to get a haircut or a shapeup. I wanted the people to see me as some crazed man who had psychological issues. I sat down on the bottom bunk to gather my thoughts. I might've acted like I hated Paris, but I still loved her ass, I just had a fucked-up way of showing it. She was the only female to ever hold me down and have my back. Even when my own mother dipped on me, Paris was right there giving me the love that I needed.

To be honest, I held a lot of animosity towards women due to my mother abandoning me. I felt like majority of women weren't shit and were only out for themselves. For the little bit of time that my mother was a part of my life, I watched the drugs destroy her. My father did any and everything in the world to please her, yet it still wasn't enough. While my father was at work being the bread winner of the family, my mother was in their bed selling her body to the highest bidder. She had a love for two of the deadliest drugs around; heroine and crack. I don't know what hurt me more, the fact that she was hooked or when she would make me shoot the dope in her because she was too sick to do it herself.

"Dixon," the fat husky looking guard called out. I couldn't stand this nigga. He was one of those correctional officers who insisted on making your stay a living hell no matter how much you abided by the rules. I swear one of these days he was gonna catch me on one of my off days and end up getting wrecked. I sized the nigga up as I went to see what he wanted.

"You can go ahead and cut all that slick ass eyeballing shit out," he said.

"What the fuck is good?" I asked. He needed to understand that him wearing that uniform meant nothing to me. Once he went home and changed into his street clothes, he was just like me; another black man that society didn't give a fuck about.

"Get cha ass out here and let's go." I bucked at him one time just to call his bluff. He was scared shitless. I laughed as I walked out of my cell until I felt him hit me in

the back of my head with his nightstick. I swear I wanted to go toe to toe with him at that moment. If I wasn't on my way to court right now, they would've been transporting him to ICU and me down to solitary confinement. I let him get his rocks off with that bitch move. We would be seeing each other sooner than later.

I swear the whole damn hood was in the court room when I entered. It didn't make no sense how nosey people were. What made it so bad was half the bitches here didn't even fuck with Paris. They only came to have something to gossip about later. I saw Paris sitting down in the front row and decided to fuck with her mind a little bit. I blew her a few kisses just to piss her nigga off. He needed to know that I hadn't forgotten about him shooting me in the nuts. I gave Romeo an ice-cold stare. Paris might've chosen him over me, but she would forever be mine. Women never got over their first real love.

Twenty minutes into the trial, the judge had called for recess. Paris played her role well when she got on the stand and testified. I smirked during her entire testimony. When she told the jurors, she had been with me for these years and had never seen this side of me, they looked at one another like it was some bullshit. Majority of the time I wasn't even listening to her story. The only thing I was interested in was hearing their decision. My lawyer had advised me to show no emotion when Paris was giving her account of what happened. But what he failed to realize was I paid him to make sure I got off and nothing else. He could keep all his advice to himself.

"We've reached our verdict," I smiled when I thought about how I planned on terrorizing Paris once I was released. The shit would've never come to this if she had just accepted that I cheated. But nah, she wanted to throw hot water on a nigga and give away all my shit.

"Legend Dixon, we find you guilty in the attempted murder of Paris Johnson. Therefore, you have been sentenced to thirty years which you will begin serving immediately."

"This is some bullshit!" I threw everything off the table, throwing chairs into the direction of Paris and Romeo. "I paid you good money and this was all that you could come up with." I released my frustration on my now ex-lawyer. He had sworn him, and the judge had already talked this shit over. I guess once the money was in his bank account all that went out the window. Whether I got off or not, he was still getting paid. The guards in the courtroom were no match for the energy that I had. The adrenaline rush I had only amped me up even more. I was knocking guards out like a beast.

"Bitch this isn't over. You'll be seeing me again," I called out to Paris.

"If you even think about coming after her, I will kill you myself!" Romeo said. This nigga was always coming to her aide like he ran shit. Romeo thought he was the only one who had a squad of niggas behind him. All I had to do was make one phone call and his ass would be touched. I had people all over this country, so if I wanted to get at him, I could really make it happen.

"My nigga you bleed just like I do. Don't think your ass is untouchable."

Romeo didn't say a word. He just nodded his head at the death threat I had just sent his way. "Every time you go to sleep I hope I haunt you in your dreams," I said to Paris. I picked up another chair and threw it her way. She ducked down right as the chair flew over her head. I dropped down to the floor once I felt a strange feeling come over me. My body stiffened up like a board. I lost the ability to speak for a few minutes. The thirty seconds I was tased felt like a lifetime.

I was alone in a room with no walls and nothing but a hard metal bed. The warden had stripped away all my privileges for the way I carried on in the courtroom. When the reality of me doing twenty-five years set in, I lost it. I had tied a sheet around my neck and tried to kill myself. It was the sucka way out, but right now it was better than being restrained in a chair with no clothes on. For the next twenty-four hours I was placed on suicide watch.

Luckily for me I had a smooth ass talk game. When one of the female officers came in to check on me, I sold her some shit about how good she looked and anything else I could think of to get inside of her head. It didn't take long for it to swell her head up. When everything was said and done, I had her making phone calls and passing messages along to my people. I even promised to give her some dick and money once I got out of the hole. I laughed on the inside at how pathetic these bitches were. All you had to do was tell them some shit that sounded good, and just like that, they were believing it. As gullible as this bitch was, I was sure I could sweet talk her into sneaking some narcotics into the prison. I had to have money coming in way. I couldn't survive in here eating that nasty shit they served as food. For the

time being I planned on doing my time while coming up with a master plan to get the hell out of here. I didn't give a damn what the judge said, I wasn't serving nobody's twenty-five years.

Chapter Fifteen

Paris

It had been well over two months since the drama had unfolded with Legend inside the courtroom. I was finally free and living my life. The dealership was up and running and things were going great between Romeo and me. Working with Romeo would take some getting used to. I hated when I saw other women in his face, but I knew it was all business. I wasn't about to mess up something he worked so hard for with my jealousy. As long as it stayed professional, I wouldn't get out of line. But best believe I would check one of these hoes real quick if they got out of line.

I looked at the clock and saw that it was just about time for me to do a lunch run. It was the last Friday of the month and Romeo was buying everyone who worked in the building lunch for being professional and team players. I went over the order sheet one last time to make sure everyone's order was correct. Once everything was verified, I placed my Gucci sunglasses on my face to block out the sun that waited for me outdoors.

I was cruising down the road, bopping my head to the music when I thought I saw a familiar car. I brushed it off when I looked in the mirror and saw that it wasn't there. I was tired, and my mind was playing tricks with me. "You have a call from your mother," my phone notified me. I eased up off the gas pedal so that I could answer the phone

"Good afternoon Sunshine. How are you?"

I chimed into the phone. I hadn't talked to my mother all week and I was happy to hear from her. I didn't want her to think that I was dodging her phone calls. With being the manager of the shop, I stayed busy a lot. Once I got home all my time and attention was devoted to my man. Now don't get me wrong, we both pulled our weight equally. Everything in our relationship was divided equally. We both cooked, cleaned, and paid the bills. Romeo had expressed his feelings about him feeling like less of a man because he wasn't providing everything. I tried to explain to him that I was independent. No matter how much a man wanted to take care of me, I would never allow him to do it completely.

"I'm good baby. I haven't heard from you in a while, so I figured I would call and see how things were going on your end."

"Everything is fine," I responded.

"How's my future son in-law?" Couldn't nobody tell her that a wedding wasn't somewhere in our future. For some reason she had taken a strong liking to Romeo. She had accepted him into our family with open arms. There wasn't anything bad she could say about a man who took care of her daughter. He treated me like a queen and in return, he got the treatments that were only meant for a king. When we laid in bed at night, I felt like I was next to Superman. There was no other place I wanted to be besides in his arms. He was my superhero, and couldn't nobody tell me anything different.

"He's doing fine," I giggled.

"If you are doing all that into the phone then he must be doing fine."

"I'm surprised you aren't sitting up watching your soap operas."

"Oh I am. If I miss anything I'll just rewind it back on the DVR. Ain't nothing about these shows ever going to change. You're always going to have that one female on the show that done slept with everybody, passing her goodies around to any man that will take it freely."

"You're a mess."

"I'm hoping to see the two of you at Sunday dinner, even in church," she said. I caught the hint she was throwing and decided to take her up on her offer. It had been a while since I'd been in the house of the Lord and I had a lot to thank him for.

"We'll be there."

"Great," she said. "Oh, your Aunt Netti and Destiny will be joining us too, along with her friend Sharnese and their spouses so please try to make it."

"I will. Look ma, I'm driving, and I need to get off this phone before I mess around and get a ticket fooling with you."

"I love you take care."

"I love you too mom," I ended the call and focused my attention back on the road. This time I knew my eyes weren't deceiving me when I saw Jade's car pulling out of the parking lot. With me being in the new car, I knew she wouldn't be able to detect it was me. I pulled over on the side of the road. I acted like something was wrong with my car and put on my emergency lights. I waited until she was well ahead of me before pulling back onto the road. Once I was sure that we were alone on the road, I smashed down on the pedal and rammed into the back of her car. Her car did doughnuts in the road, but somehow, she was able to gain control.

I was livid. Jade was one of those people that could do so much wrong and, yet the Lord still spared her life. I ran into the back of her car for the second time. I

was determined to have her in a casket before today was over. I wanted payback in the worst way. It was so close I could taste it on my lips.

A wicked smile spread across my face when her car went flying into a ditch. It was crazy how not one car had rode past yet. I wasn't complaining though. I didn't need anybody coming to her aide. I ran over to see what condition she was in. I was disgusted to see only a minor cut on her forehead. I swear this bitch either had nine lives or she was immortal.

"I bet I'm the last person you're expecting to see," I said as I grabbed her by her hair. She tried to pull me down with her, but I held my balance. I had been in the gym getting fit, so the hits that she attempted to throw were nothing.

Jade laughed in my face as if something was real funny. I slapped her ass one good time. Instantly the smirk on her face was removed. She always thought everything was a game. She cared about nobody but herself. The number of people she had hurt through her life was endless, and it would only grow if someone didn't get rid of her.

"Actually, I've been waiting to run into you. I see you healed very well," she busted out laughing at her own words. I knew then that Jade needed some serious mental help.

"What is it Jade? What did I ever do to you? Was I not a friend like you wanted? I mean, please let me know what I did to deserve the bullshit that you did?" I wanted to know what made her turn her back on me. Jade knew if she ever needed anything, then I was always there. I was the one who helped pick her up when her family let her down. There were times when I even let her stay in my house when she got put out of her own. I still couldn't believe she'd gone behind my back like that. We were supposed to be sisters until the end, but here we were; enemies at war with each other.

The more I thought about it, the more I realized Jade was a fucked-up individual. There was something inside of her that she was struggling to deal with. You never knew a person's entire story. For some reason, I couldn't bring myself to do any more harm to this girl. She wasn't worth me going to jail or losing my sanity. I no longer had the energy to deal with any negativity. By no means was I forgiving her for the things that she'd done, I was just allowing her to live another day, but only for the sake of her daughter. There were already too many children growing up in this cold world without parents.

"Consider yourself lucky today."

"I always said you were nothing but a soft-hearted bitch. The only strong points you possess are being under Sanai's ass all the time, which is why I don't regret fucking Legend or Knowledge. I forgot to tell you that he begged me to have his baby."

"I'm not the least bit surprised. In case you haven't noticed, Knowledge has kids all over Brooklyn."

"No darling, I'm talking about Legend." She had a nerve to emphasize by rubbing her belly. My eyes darted towards her stomach. She did have a slight pudge, but I didn't think much of it since she'd always had a gut. The words of the doctor telling me that I may never be able to have kids played in my head. All the shit I'd said earlier about saving her life went out the window. I tried to charge at her, but was too late. Jade sent a few blows to my body which sent me flying back on the car. I fought to catch my breath, but Jade was still delivering blow after blow.

"See this where y'all bitches got me fucked up at. I never gave a fuck about none of y'all. I've been plotting on you hoes for a minute. You and Sanai always walked around like y'all were hot shit, while I walked around as the third wheel. But those days are long gone. Now it's my time to shine."

"That's what all this is about, you're jealous?" Everything she said made sense. All the signs of her being jealous were always there, but I never paid them any attention. I was too busy being a good friend, something she knew nothing about. No wonder she insisted that I have an abortion, and like a fool I listened, thinking she was being sincere. In the midst of listening to Jade talk, I

let my guard down and she was able to wrap her hands around my throat. Jade pushed me into the driver's window. The glass shattered, and I could feel the blood running down my face. I reached into her car for anything I could use as a weapon. Jade was getting the best of me and I refused to go out without a fight. With the crowbar in hand, I used my weight to pull myself up and came out swinging. I went across it with her face knocking her ass out. No matter how hard I tried to be nice, she insisted on ticking me off.

Jade was laid on the ground holding the side of her face. The way I was feeling I didn't give a damn if she bled to death. I didn't plan on saving her life this go around. I grabbed her feet and dragged her body out into the woods.

"I hope you die out here and the animals have a good time eating away at your body," I said as I walked off leaving her to suffer. Killing her would not have given me the satisfaction that I wanted. I'd rather her die a slow death so that she could feel the pain that she had caused everyone around her. I walked back to her car and set it on fire. My phone vibrated in my pocket. Romeo was texting to see if I had gotten everyone's food. I was so occupied with Jade I had forgotten all about it. I jumped into my car and went to go pick up everyone's lunch. I would just tell them some bogus story about how it wasn't prepared.

♥♥♥♥♥♥

"Sorry I'm late everyone," I said as I handed everyone in the breakroom their lunch. I got a few looks from a few of my co-workers, but I couldn't even check them on it since I was the one in the wrong.

"Late? Girl, lunchtime is over," said one of my coworkers named India. She was popping her gum and had the whole neck rolling thing going on. She was a cute girl and all, but sometimes she got too fly out of the mouth for my liking.

"Well, since I am the manager, lunchtime has been extended by another hour. Now does that make up for me being late?" I asked.

Everybody clapped their hands and cheered. Any ill feelings they had disappeared when they realized they still had another free hour to themselves. After making sure everyone was satisfied, I went into my office to collect my thoughts. My mind kept wandering back to Jade. I was one of those people who couldn't do much wrong without my heart turning soft. I turned on the lights in the bathroom to give myself a full examination. In the car I had cleaned up most of the blood on my face. I was glad nobody noticed it. I applied a little bit of foundation to cover the scars that Jade had left. When I

came out the bathroom, Romeo was standing at the window with a big folder in his hands.

"I need you to go over everything in here and have it turned in before you leave today."

"No problem. Just sit them on my desk and I'll get straight to it."

"Good looking ma. And I'ma need you to go over these resumes so that we can get some more help around here."

"With the way business is booming, and with holidays coming up, we're going to need the extra help, especially on the sales floor."

"I was thinking about doing an incentive every month to increase the sales. Something that will give them the motivation to work even harder."

"It just might work since everybody around here is all about getting them coins."

"You alright?" he asked, looking at me funny.

"Tired for the most part." I hated lying to Romeo, but I knew he would've went off if I told him what had just taken place between me and Jade. Romeo wanted to be my savior, but some situations I had to handle on my own. If I got comfortable with letting him be in control of everything, what would I do when it came time for me to depend on myself? Just because we were together today, it didn't mean we would still be with each other come tomorrow. Without or without him, I needed to stand on my own two feet. Nothing lasted forever these days, and I wanted to be prepared just in case I ended up alone.

"If you need to leave early go ahead and I'll just meet you at the house."

"Thanks bae, I'ma try to stick it out." Working with Romeo was easier than I expected it to be. While we were at work we kept things professional. Everyone here knew we were a couple, but we didn't show it. I didn't have time to be dealing with those co-workers who felt like I was treated differently.

I went over the resumes of a few potential candidates. I really didn't care what was typed up on paper; I needed to see these people in person so that I could feel them out. Just because a person had experience in an area, it didn't make them qualified for the job. I was even willing to work with the ones who had little or no experience at all; everybody had to start somewhere. I placed phone calls to the ones that piqued my interest. I planned on giving everyone a fair chance, but there were a few that caught my eye. After scheduling their interviews for Monday morning, I locked up my desk and went to go check on Romeo. When I reached the front desk, he was occupied with a big breasted Spanish broad. I didn't care that they were conversing; it was his place of business. But what I had a problem with was her rubbing her hands up and down his arm. She didn't have to touch him to get her point across. I pranced over to him with the fakest smile I could master up.

"Excuse me for one second," he said to the woman who acted like she had an attitude because I interrupted their conversation.

"What's wrong baby?" he asked. The scent of his cologne filled my nose. This man was my weakness. He was just like poison, hazardous to my health, but I just had to have him. He was my deadly addiction.

"I just came to tell you I was leaving."

"Can you hurry up; my time is very valuable. If you don't know how to conduct business I can take my money and spend it somewhere more professional." No, this rude ass heifer didn't. I looked at Romeo and he nodded his head, giving me the signal to check her real quick. I counted to ten inside of my head. I wanted to remain as professional as possible. There were still other customers in the building.

"If that's how you feel then you can kindly exit the building and never return," I said, pointing my figure towards the exit. She looked at Romeo in confusion.

"And you are?" she asked with her nose turned up in the air. I could've cared less about her attitude. What I didn't like was her disrespect. All she had to do was wait five minutes, but she insisted on being a jackass.

"I just happen to be the manager and his spouse," I said, throwing it out there just to see her reaction. One thing I couldn't stand was a bitch that felt like they could treat people any kind of way because they had money. "Oh, so you're one of those?"

"Excuse me?" I replied, not sure of what she was getting at. All I knew was my patience was running extremely thin with this broad.

"One of those gold digging bitches that use men for their money."

"You need to get off my property before I call the police and have them remove you," Romeo said. I was glad he had come to her rescue. Things were about to make a turn for the worse had she kept on running her mouth.

"You mean to tell me you're about to let all of this money go down the drain over her?" the woman looked at me in disgust. I was just about to respond when Romeo grabbed my hand.

"Don't worry let me handle this," he said, pushing me to the side.

"I don't tolerate anyone disrespecting my lady, I don't care how much money you're spending. They didn't stop making U.S. currency or any other form of money when they made yours. Now I'm not going to tell you again to leave the premises."

"I'll be sure to report this company to the better business bureau and rant about your customer service. Someone must've forgotten to tell you that the customer is always right, no matter what the circumstance is."

"You can tell Obama while you're at it, I don't give a damn." I was proud of the way he handled the situation. I wasn't sure I would've been able to remain that calm.

"Thank you," I said to him.

"It was nothing. That bitch had been working my nerves since she walked into the door, demanding shit like she was the Queen of England. I'm glad to have her ass up out of here."

"I can imagine." Today's events had drained the life out of me. I was ready to go home and put one or two in the air. I needed to unwind and get my mind right. It would've been even better if Romeo came home and surprised me with some bomb ass sex. I had a lot of tension in my body that I felt the need to release. It was the weekend and I was ready to turn up in the comfort of my own home with my man.

Chapter Sixteen

Jade

It didn't matter how many times I got my ass whooped; I would stop at nothing to get my revenge. Paris was feeling real salty when I told her I was having Legend's baby. The look on her face was worth a million dollars. She would never admit it, but deep down inside she was wishing she'd kept that baby.

If a hunter hadn't been in the woods hunting, I would've been dead. The temperature had dropped, and it was freezing out. With all the moaning I had been doing the man and his two sons had mistaken me for a wild animal. They offered to take me to the hospital, but I declined their services. All I needed was a heating blanket and some Aspirin. I was tired of going to the hospital every time something happened, and I wasn't in the mood to answer a bunch of questions that I was sure they would ask. I had them drop me off at the nearest hotel. Right now, I was in no condition to head home; I just wanted to soak my body in some hot water. The injuries weren't as bad as I thought they would be. My ribcage was on fire from where Paris had kicked me. If I was indeed pregnant, the baby was long gone, which didn't matter to me. Legend could do nothing for me locked away behind bars.

Somewhere along the lines Legend started thinking I was his girl and that it was my job to take care and provide for his every need, and that's where he had me confused with Paris. Taking care of a grown man was not on my agenda. I could do bad my damn self. If he couldn't bring anything to the table, I didn't need him around. Legend and his constant threats resulted in me getting a restraining order on his ass. When I found out it was his baby mama that turned him in, I laughed like there was no tomorrow. He had played Paris for another bitch, and in return, he got played by that bitch. I stepped into the bathtub and eased my aching muscles. The hot water brought me back around. I knew I would have to take it easy for a few days. I needed time to heal. Paris and Sanai both had some shit headed their way. I was the one who started all of this, and I planned on finishing it. In the end, I would be the only one left standing. Didn't they realize that no matter how hard they tried to get rid of me it was impossible? All my life I had been fighting to get the happiness that I felt I deserved. Did it make me feel better by hurting other people? Yes and no. Nobody around me understood what I dealt with daily. Hell, I didn't even understand it. I was beginning to think that my mother was right about me needing to seek professional help, but it would never happen. I wasn't about to spill my life story and emotions out to a person that didn't give a damn about my well-being. Most shrinks were only concerned about getting their money. With the amount they charged, I could be my own psychiatrist.

My mind wandered back to Knowledge. At one time I really thought I had a chance at being his girl. He made it seem like I raped him and that was the end of it. He acted like we didn't spend time together on a daily basis. Well it might not have been daily, but it was more than a one-night stand like he portrayed. If he would've come clean to Sanai in the beginning like I told him, we wouldn't even be dealing with this shit. If Sanai could accept the fact that he had gotten other bitches pregnant while they were together then she could accept this too. I wasn't the first bitch he cheated with, and with his track record, I was certain I wouldn't be the last. I let the water out the tub and turned on the shower to revive myself with some hot water. With my surgery right around the corner, I couldn't keep bringing all this harm to my body.

Paris should've killed me when she had the chance. She had made the worst mistake of her life by letting me live. A knock at the door startled me out of my thoughts. Nobody except the men from earlier knew where I was at. The only reason I hadn't contacted my mother was because I wasn't in the mood to hear her mouth. Every time we engaged in a conversation she felt the need to lecture me about how I wasn't living my life right. Growing up, I was always treated as the black sheep of the family. My mother's only concern was my older sister. She always bragged about how smart and beautiful she was, but always considered me to be the problem child. I might've acted out all the time, but it was only because I wasn't getting the attention that I needed so I started manipulating people to get whatever I felt my heart desired. The lack of love I received from my mother led to me being envious of the relationships other people had with each other.

I threw my clothes on and looked in the peephole. It was the men that brought me here. I didn't know what they could possibly want with me, so I remained quiet. I was in no condition to defend myself in case they wanted to try something stupid. They knocked for another five minutes before finally giving up. I went to window and peeked from the side of the curtain to make sure they were gone. Once I saw their car leave out the parking lot, I cut everything off in the room and climbed into the bed. This was one of the main reasons I hated staying in cheap hotels, they lacked a good security system. I plugged my phone into the wall so that it would be fully charged. Come the morning time I was getting the hell out of here just in case those men decided to come back.

♥♥♥♥♥♥

I was depressed as hell looking at the receipt with my account balance on it. Being broke was not something I was used to. I had six hundred dollars to my name and I needed to make some happen, and quick. Not being able to work at the club had put a huge strain on me financially. I depended on my face and body to provide me with my lavish lifestyle. I was a hustler by heart. It wouldn't be long before I was back to my usual self. I was scrolling through the posts on Facebook when I came across Tamika, my first cousin on my mother's side. She stayed with a sick scheme. Her boyfriend was one of the biggest jack boy's around the way. Torien only robbed dope boys that were getting that dough. He didn't waste his time with petty hustlers who only sold dime and nick bags. Whenever word got out that he was in town, everybody closed shop and setup out of town. I sent her a message with my number telling her to hit me up when she got a chance. Five minutes had barely passed and already she was calling.

"Damn that was fast," I said to myself.

"Hey Mika," I sang into the phone. Just like me, she was all about her money.

Hey boo," she replied back. "If you're calling me, then you must be ready to put in some work."

"And I know you got some work for me."

"How much cash you trying to make so that I know what kind of mission to send you on. Some quick loop for tonight or something that's gonna last you awhile?"

"I ain't gonna lie, my pockets looking real empty right now," I said coming clean. I know you got something that'll have me right for a good while."

"Come to think of it, I do, but it's going down tonight. I'm sure you're more than aware of what Torien does. The only thing I need for you to do is pretend that you're trying to trick with Taz. You do know who he is right?"

"Of course, I do. Taz had every girl in the club trying to make him sponsor them. He was one of the big spenders that came through on a regular. He stayed blessing the stage with his dirty money."

"This should be a piece of cake for you then. Your main goal is to end up back at his crib before the sun comes up. What you do to get there is your business. Fuck this up, and Torien will be on ya ass. He won't care that me and you are blood."

"You done ran everything down except one thing."
"And what's that?" she asked like she didn't already know.

"How much is he paying for this? I need to know that the price is right before I go committing myself to anything."

"Since this is a big lick, he's starting the price at ten thousand. That's only if no mishaps occur. I need you to be on point and focused. If by any chance you don't feel that you can complete the task at hand, let me know now so that I can find another girl to do the job."

I needed this money more than anything right now, but I also knew how Torien got down. If things didn't go the way he planned, I would be missing come sunrise. I wasn't the least bit surprised about Taz being their target. He stayed wearing flashy clothes and jewelry while bragging about how much money he had.

"This shit ain't nothing to a boss," I replied sounding rather cocky, but it was true. Seducing niggas was what I did best. I knew all the right things to do to make a nigga come out of their pockets.

"Put on the sluttiest outfit you can find and make sure your hair and makeup is slayed. I need you to be on your best bullshit. If you gonna come half-stepping I won't hesitate to replace you with someone else."

I listened to my cousin give out orders like she was my pimp. She just needed to play her position while I went to work. She was acting like I was a rookie at getting money, when fucking niggas for money was what I did.

"I got this. All I need for you to do is give me the name and directions of the club."

"Now that I can't do, but I will pick you up at ten. We may be family and all, but I don' trust you. I haven't heard from you in forever and out of the blue you hit me up wanting to make some money. No offense, but that shit real suspect to me." I couldn't disagree with anything that Mika was saying. I would've felt the same way.

"No hard feelings. I'm just trying to come up, that's all."

"Good, now that we have an understanding, give me your address so that I know where to pick you up from." I went ahead and told her my address. We talked for a few minutes bringing each other up to speed, you know typical hood gossip. I called a cab to take me to the mall. I needed to find a banging outfit that would catch Taz's eyes. Since my funds were on the low side I would have to style my own hair. I wasn't worried about the makeup since I did my own anyway. If everything went as planned tonight, I would have all the money I needed for my surgery.

Chapter Seventeen

Sanai

I rolled over to see who kept calling my phone like they were crazy. I still had another thirty minutes before I had to get up and get the kids ready for school. I caught an attitude when I saw that Knowledge was the cause of me not getting my full eight hours of sleep. I hit the silence button on the phone. Right now, I wasn't in the mood to deal with his bullshit. Every day he was sending me the same tired message about how he needed me in his life to feel complete.

If I didn't get any entertainment from anybody else, I definitely got it from him. I got out of bed and pulled the covers back. It would have to do until I came back to wash the sheets. I washed my face and brushed my teeth before going to wake the kids up. To my surprise, they were already in the kitchen eating a bowl of cereal. I smiled when I looked at the two of them. My babies weren't babies anymore. They were growing up on me, but they would always be considered my babies.

"Good morning," I said to them. They paid me no mind as they were caught up in their morning shows. "I said, good morning." This time I stood in front of the TV, so they had no choice but to acknowledge me. "Good morning, mommy," they both replied together. Justice had an attitude that I wasn't feeling, and I had an idea as to where it was coming from.

"Justice what's wrong with you this morning?"

"When is daddy coming home?" she asked, I swallowed real hard. I wasn't prepared to have this conversation with my six-year-old.

"I don't know baby. Daddy and mommy need sometime apart right now."

"Well I miss him, and I want him to come home." Justice was a straight daddy's girl. Her world consisted of her and Knowledge. Every night he would read her a book and tuck her in, it was their way of bonding. Knowledge had her spoiled rotten. Anything she asked for he made it his business to make it happen. But he was that way with all his kids. When it came to being a good man he wasn't shit, but he was a good father and I couldn't take that away from him.

The ringing of the doorbell saved me from having to respond to Justice. It was too early in the morning for company, and I wasn't expecting any deliveries. When I opened the door, I was greeted with several different color roses.

"I have a delivery for a Miss Sanai."

"That would be me," I replied.

"Can you sign here for me?" He handed me a pen so that I could sign for the roses. "Where would you like us to place the rest of them?"

"There's more?" He moved to the side, and sure enough the yard was flooded. I had no idea where I would put all of them; they damn sure weren't coming in the house.

"I'll be right back." I ran into the living room to get my wallet. "How much will it cost me to have you deliver some of these to all of my neighbors around here? You can even give them some story about me thanking them for being such good neighbors."

"You're serious, aren't you?" he asked.

"As serious as a heart attack."

"Don't you at least want to know who sent them to you?" I grabbed the white card from out of his hand. When I saw that it was from Knowledge I started not to read it, but I went ahead and opened it anyway. My eyes swelled up with tears as I read the note. Knowledge was expressing his love for me like he should've done a long time ago. He was finally admitting to his wrongs and taking full responsibility for them, which was something he had never done before. Normally he always had that 'I don't give a fuck if you leave or stay' mind frame. I wanted to believe that Knowledge was ready to be the man that I knew he could be, but I wasn't in the business of getting hurt again. We had been down this road several times before, only for him to do good for a few months and then turn around and go back to his old ways. "Mommy, why are you crying?" asked my son Jordan. To be so young, he was always trying to protect me. I knew he would one day grow up and become a wonderful man.

"I just read something that made me happy on the inside." I rubbed the top of his head as he clung to my leg. "Go ahead and finish your breakfast, the bus will be here any minute."

"Whoever sent you these must really love you."

"What makes you so sure?" I asked.

"I'm not sending no woman a bunch of roses if she doesn't mean anything to me. Nowadays you can't find a man that is even thinking about being romantic. Most men are only concerned with what's between your legs. Nobody's gonna go out of their way unless they done really fucked up."

"You have no idea." I gave him two hundred dollars and told him to clean up my yard. I waved goodbye to the kids as they got on the bus. Kisses were no longer allowed as they left for school. They told me I was embarrassing them in front of their friends. Once I saw the bus pull off, I went into the house to clean up the mess they had left behind.

I turned the channel to the *Maury Povich* show. It was nothing but the usual on the show. A bunch of ratchet females claiming that they had only had sex with one man, knowing damn well that there were at least three other men who could've possibly fathered their kids. But some of the men on here weren't any better. They would have fifty million reasons why they couldn't be the father when the child looked exactly like him.

I went into the utility room to start up the washer. It was my least favorite day of the week. I hated having to wash clothes and then put them up too. I ran up the steps to the bedroom and pulled the sheets off the bed. My phone was on the nightstand steady going off. I looked on the screen and I had fifty missed calls in the last five minutes from Knowledge. He was doing too much this morning. I needed to get myself together before I dealt with him.

Me: I'll call you when I get some time. Right now, I am busy.

Knowledge: I'll be there in two hours.

Me: No, I'll call you when I'm ready. Don't press your luck.

Knowledge: I hear you.

Knowledge knew how to get on my nerves with his arrogant ass. He insisted on having things his way. Even though I had specifically told him I would call him when I was ready, in his head it meant twenty minutes. I grabbed my washcloth and body wash from out of the closet and went to take care of my hygiene. I wasted no time scrubbing my body down good. I always paid extra attention to my private area. I couldn't understand how some of these females walked around smelling of a mixture between fish and musk. I was in the shower humming along to the sounds of Jazmine Sullivan's "Mascara" when the shower curtains were snatched back.

"You in here feeling on ya self and shit, no wonder you don't hear me knocking on the door." Knowledge must've been nearby the entire time. He probably was watching to see my reaction when I received the roses.

"Then you should've waited until I came to the door. Since I didn't give you permission to enter, what you did would be considered trespassing."

"Trespassing my ass. My money when into this house, or did you forget? Now turn around so that I can wash ya back." Knowledge smirked at me and then licked his lips. He knew I would become weak once I felt his touch. I rolled my eyes at him and handed him the washcloth.

"This doesn't mean you're back on my good side," I said, letting him know that he wasn't running this show.

"Can a nigga just do something nice for once without having to hear ya mouth? Just relax and let me do this."

He took his time washing the soap from off my back. Each time I felt his touch my clit tingled. I closed my eyes as his hands roamed over my body. Knowledge pulled me away from the showerhead as he caressed my breasts. He played with my nipples as they turned rock hard.

"Ahh." I didn't mean for the moan to come out of my mouth. It had been a minute since I last had some sexual healing.

"You like that, don't you?" Knowledge said. He used his fingers to play with my pearl and I lost it. I rocked my hips back and forth as I felt my wetness slide down on his fingers. I was dripping like a waterfall.

"What are you doing to me Knowledge?" He said nothing as he rubbed on my clit some more. Knowledge wiped away my juices. I was breathing real heavy from just that mini session. Knowledge helped me out of the shower and into the bedroom.

"You know Sanai, with us being apart I had some time to think, and it fucked me up when I realized how bad I've treated you over the years. There is no excuse for my actions. I dogged you out when you were the one who stood in my corner. You were with me when I didn't have shit and I let the money go to my head. I took ya love for granted and I'm sorry."

Knowledge was down on his knees expressing his love for me. My heart softened up when I saw that his eyes were wet. The only time I had ever seen him cry was the time we buried Juju.

"I told you, you would miss all of my good loving. You know that my love is like crack. No matter how hard you try to shake me you can't get me out of your system. I ain't gonna lie that shit with you and Jade cut me deep. I

thought we were passed the cheating and the side kids. As much as I want to give you a second chance I don't feel that you're worthy of my love. I done put so much into this relationship only for you to give me your ass to kiss. We done been together for too many years to throw this shit away. All I want is for us to get our shit together. I'm not trying to be thirty still going through the same shit with you. If we're gonna be in this together then there's going to be some changes around here."

Knowledge was not about to step foot back in this house until we reached an agreement. I was tired of playing games with him. Either he was ready to step up and be a man, or I was going to find someone else to fill his spot.

"What kind of changes are we talking about?"

"See, let me stop you right there. You shouldn't have been asking any questions at all. The first thing that should be coming out of your mouth is what do I need to do to make things right." He huffed a little before asking the first question.

"What's the first thing, Sanai?"

"I'ma need for you to start pulling your weight around here when it comes to these kids. It's not easy taking care of them and running a business at the same time. The least you can do is help them get ready for school in the morning, and helping out with homework."

"No problem, what's next?"

"If you see that I'm busy, get dinner started. Jordan and Justice can't cook for themselves just yet." "Got it. Any more demands?" he asked.

"Of course, I do! If you think it's gonna be that easy then you got another thing coming. You ought to be thanking Jordan and Justice for my mind change. If you could've seen the looks they've been wearing on their faces for the last few weeks. You being away from the house has really affected them. I've noticed the change in Justice's behavior since you haven't been around. If that child doesn't love nobody else, she definitely loves her daddy."

I was willing to give our relationship another try for the sake of the kids. But as far as me trusting him when it came to other females, it would take some time.

"Let me be real clear with what I'm about to say. Any fuck ups and we're done for good. I shouldn't even be giving you another chance as it is. I'm not putting up with none of your shit this go around. The coming in late in the morning stops. You better have all of your business completed at a decent time."

"We'll talk about my business another time. I got all your requests. I see now I'm going to be walking around here on pins and needles." he laughed, but I didn't find a thing funny.

"Come over here and give me some of that good stuff that I've been missing."

"Nigga, if you want some of this here, you're going to have to come get it." I dropped my robe to the floor. Knowledge approached me, and I placed both of my hands-on top of the dresser. I spread my legs apart and arched my back to the best of my ability. Right now, I just wanted a quickie. I wasn't in the mood for the loving making. I had an itch that needed to be scratched.

"Let's make it do what it does. Knowledge I ain't got all day, I got stuff to do." Knowledge rammed his dick in me so hard I had no choice but to choke up. My mouth always got me in trouble when it came to his dick game.

"Don't stop talking now, keep on talking shit," Knowledge said. He watched his dick slide in and out of my pussy. The sounds of his balls smacking against my ass were the only sounds I was interested in now.

"Damn I missed this dick," I hollered out. Knowledge was putting in work and making up for lost time.

"Show me you missed it."

On cue I bounced back to his rhythm. I threw my ass hard, letting him know I wasn't playing any games. Knowledge knew I was a pro when it came to taking dick. Never would you find me running from it.

"You been giving my pussy away?" he asked. I ignored him and continued to throw this ass in a circle.

"So, you can't hear now." He pounded so deep I felt his dick in my stomach. If he wanted an answer from me he would have to beat it up out of me. "I said, have you been giving my pussy away?"

"No," I cried, the dick was just too good. I reached my hand between my legs and squeezed his balls.

"Hmm," he moaned. "Come on and cum with me," he said, biting down into my shoulder. Before I could respond I felt Knowledge shoot his seeds inside of me. The sex reminded me of why I had fallen in love with him in the first place. Knowledge had that bomb dick.

"Does this mean that I get my key back?"

"Hell no, you got to work for that. The first few nights back you'll have to sleep in the guest room. I might've just fucked you, but I'm not ready to share a bed with you just yet."

"Why you got to be playing like that?" he said.

"If you think this is a game you can kindly return to Juju's house. That's right nigga, I know everything."

"Calm down girl, I was just fucking with you. Get out ya damn feelings."

It did feel good having Knowledge back around. He was the only person that could still make me smile, even when I was mad at his ass. I only hoped I wasn't making a huge mistake by letting him back in my life. For the time being I would give him the benefit of the doubt, but I planned on clocking his every move. It would take some time for him to earn all my trust back. Right now, I planned on taking things one day at a time. I planned on telling Knowledge that he had to get a paternity test for all his kids. I had gotten one done on the twins, so there wasn't any reason the rest of them couldn't get one. If we were going to be together then we needed to get rid of any loose strings. I had a funny feeling a few of these kids would come out not to be his.

Chapter Eighteen

Jade

I looked myself over in the mirror at least a million times. The surgeon had done one mean ass job on the new and improved me. I swear I looked like I could've been Sanai's long-lost sister. Not only did he enhance my features, but he also gave me a Brazilian butt lift and breast implants while he was at it. I was already bad before, but now I was really feeling myself. Shit, for twenty thousand everything had better come out right. I had sucked and fucked too many dicks to get that kind of loot, so everything had better be worth the money. I walked out of the bathroom and took my seat in the waiting room. I was here for my six weeks visit to make sure that everything had healed properly. So far, I hadn't had any problems, but I wanted to be on the safe side.

I looked down at my phone hoping to see a message or missed call from Knowledge, but my notifications were blank. It had been a month or two since I'd last had any contact with him, and nothing had changed as far as him claiming Asia. If anything, he still went around acting like she still didn't exist. I had finally told my mother who Asia's father was and let me tell you, she was disgusted by my actions. I swear she called me everything but a child of God, which was funny when she never even took her ass to church. Now I had done a lot of dirt, but I wasn't ashamed of nothing I had done. Our argument was so bad she went and filed for full custody of my daughter. To me it wasn't that serious. If she wanted Asia, then I was about to grant her, her wish. I packed up all of Asia's things and sent them to her. That was two months ago, and I still hadn't seen my daughter. Now being a mother was the last thing on my mind. In the last three months Paris had made two attempts to take my life, but failed. The bitch had finally grown some balls. I guess the last ass whipping that Legend had put on her had finally brought out the hood in her. Or maybe Romeo had toughened her up a little bit. Whatever it was, she'd better get her ammunition cause a war was about to go down.

"Sanai," the nurse called out my name, messing up my concentration. I was on Instagram following Paris's latest posts. She had just put up a picture of her new home. I couldn't call the location, but I knew she wasn't living in Brooklyn anymore. Grabbing my purse from out the chair next to me, I made my way to the back of the office. The nurse checked my body for any signs of infection and swelling.

"The doctor will be in to see you shortly."

"Thank you," I said before pulling out my phone to do some investigating. The picture was so far away I couldn't even see the street number. Nothing about the area looked familiar at all. The only thing I knew was that the house was in an upscale neighborhood. Since she had gotten another job, I had no way of finding out her whereabouts, but I was sure we would run into each other soon enough. Tired of lurking on her page, I threw my phone down into my purse. I was getting agitated trying to figure this shit out.

"How's everything going Jade?" the doctor asked as soon as he walked through the door. He had been nothing but a big help during the entire process. Of course, I made sure to tip him very well before the surgery had taken place. And let me be the first to say that those foreign men knew what they were doing when it came to satisfying a woman in the bedroom.

"Everything's everything. No complaints over here."

"Well that's good to hear. No depression or anything like that is there?"

"Not at all. If anything, my confidence was at an all-time high." With my new identity I felt like I was sitting on top of the world. The next thing on my list was to get a name change. That's right, when it was time for everything to go down them bitches would never see me coming.

"That's good. Are you still taking the pain medication that was prescribed?" He was starting to get on my nerves with all the questions he was asking, but I knew he was just doing his job.

"No, I flushed them all down the toilet when I noticed that the pain had gone away." I was lying. I had sold them to my old neighbor who stayed high all the time from anything she could get her hands on. At the time I was in need of some cash and that was the quickest way to make a few dollars.

"Great! Too many young people are overdosing from prescription drugs." He asked a few more questions before finally examining my body. After determining that everything was fine, he gave me a slip releasing me to my regular duties and sent me on my way. With or without his consent, I was doing what I wanted to anyway.

I went home to pack up the remainder of my things. After today no one would know where I resided, not even my own mother. I tried calling Knowledge again, but this time it said his phone had been disconnected. I knew that wasn't nothing but some bullshit. Knowledge must have gotten a new number. If only he had answered the phone, it might've stopped me from what I planned on doing next. I fixed my hair into a style that I knew Sanai would wear. After digging through the box of clothes I found the calmest outfit I could find and put it on. I practiced impersonating Sanai for at least thirty minutes. Feeling as though I had it down packed, I got in my car and made my way to P.S. 705

♥♥♥♥♥♥

My heart thumped as I walked into the school. I look around hoping that no one would recognize me, but then I remembered that I had a new look. I placed my glasses on as I opened the door.

"I'm here to pick up Jordan Santana," I said to the office administrator. She didn't even bother to look up and acknowledge me.

"Sign in over there on the clipboard." Her voice wasn't pleasant at all. I hated when females got certain job positions that made them think they were above and better than everybody else. I tapped my foot repeatedly as I waited for them to bring me Jordan. Ten minutes had passed, and she still hadn't contacted his teacher.

"Is there a problem? I mean I have been patiently waiting here for the last ten minutes." My attitude was beginning to show. If I didn't get myself under control I would end up blowing my cover.

She rolled her eyes before calling his name on the intercom. He walked in wearing that same serious look that Knowledge kept on his face.

"How's my little man doing?" I asked, trying to feel him out a little bit. I didn't know if he would scream and say he didn't know me. Luckily for me, he went along with everything.

I was surprised at how easy it was to kidnap a child while they were in the care of the school system. All I did was go into the main office and give them the name of Sanai's son. The girl at the desk didn't even ask for identification as I signed him out using Sanai's name. She was more focused on the phone conversation that she was engaged in than she was worrying about the safety of a child. I was starting to feel a little bit of remorse for getting the child involved, but oh well, the deed was done now. If I had to kidnap every one of their kids to get my point across, then I planned on doing just that.

"Are you hungry Jordan?" I asked him. He was the spitting image of his father. I imagined that's what my son would've looked like if Asia had been a boy.

"Yes," he responded. I could tell that Jordan had a lot of Sanai in him. He didn't show a bit of fear when I picked him up. I knew my voice still sounded the same, but my look was totally different. Even my own daughter was afraid of me at first.

"Okay cool. I'll take you to McDonald's and then afterwards you'll go and play with your sister Asia."

"My sister?" he asked in the cutest voice ever.

"Yes, your sister. You and Asia have the same father," I replied, knowing I was dead wrong. But since Knowledge failed to do his job, I was about to do it for him. Just because our situation was fucked up, it was no excuse for why the kids didn't know the truth. I drove to McDonald's in silence as I thought of my next plan. I wasn't sure how long I would keep Jordan. I had a desire to see both Sanai and Knowledge beg and plead for the return of their son.

To be continued